Have You Any Rogues?

Also by Elizabeth Boyle

HAVE YOU
ANY ROGUES?

A Rhymes With Love Novella

ELIZABETH BOYLE

AVONIMPULSE
An Imprint of HarperCollinsPublishers

Excerpt from *If Wishes Were Earls* copyright © 2014 by Elizabeth Boyle.

EPub Edition DECEMBER 2013 ISBN: 9780062322883

Print Edition ISBN: 9780062322906

10 9 8 7 6 5 4 3 2

To my dear husband,
my very own rogue.

HAVE YOU ANY ROGUES?

CHAPTER ONE

Never look a Seldon woman in the eye. Unless
you want to be cursed to the end of your days.

A DALE FAMILY MAXIM

Owle Park, 1810

Having put her nephew's country house in order, Lady Juniper, the former Lady Henrietta Seldon, glanced around at the Holland covers and the clean, gleaming floors and smiled.

"Everything is in order," she said to Mr. Muggins, the great big dog at her side, hoping to instill a sense of responsibility in the grand Irish terrier. Unfortunately, Mr. Muggins had a rather dismal record when it came to being orderly, and he gazed up at her as if he hadn't the least notion as to what she was talking about.

Henrietta sighed. No wonder the dog's mistress, the former Tabitha Timmons, now Duchess of Preston, had been reluctant to leave the mongrel behind—and it certainly explained Her Grace's parting words, "You don't mind taking care of him, do you? He can be a bit of a—"

Tabitha hadn't finished that sentence, for Henrietta had rushed to explain Mr. Muggins wouldn't be any trouble whatsoever.

More fated words had never been uttered.

Mr. Muggins was always trouble.

The great big unruly dog had ruined one of Henrietta's favorite feathered muffs and nearly gotten to the plumes in her best bonnet.

"Well, we are off to London any time now, and you will be Tabitha's problem once again," Henrietta told the dog.

The dog glanced around as if looking for who might be the object of such a statement.

Henrietta sighed again and looked around one last time. The only thing left to do was to have the housekeeper's son bring up the crate of wines that her nephew, Christopher Seldon, the Duke of Preston, had asked her to bring to town, then she, Mr. Muggins and her maid, Poppy, could return to London.

Though Poppy was vehemently against traveling on this night—All Hallows' Eve—claiming spirits of the past would be haunting the roads.

"Unexpected things can happen, my lady," she'd warned.

A notion Henrietta whisked aside as utter nonsense as she looked out the window at the tree-lined drive, where a scattering of fall leaves rustled across the gravel, while overhead the tenacious few leaves still clinging to the branches fluttered about in jaunty defiance of the changing seasons.

Still, Poppy's words came hauntingly back to tease her.

Unexpected things . . .

Those words rustled down Henrietta's spine with a rest-less sense of destiny—which she quickly swept aside like the dust on the bookshelves.

Restless desires no longer had any place in her life, she reminded herself.

She was a respectable widow now.

Well, if one could be so when one was no more than eight and twenty and had already buried three husbands.

Marriages made because she'd made impetuous decisions and followed impulsive desires . . .

And like the wind that pulled and tugged at the leaves, that single word, *desires*, tugged at her heart.

Oh, bother the notion, she tried telling herself.

For the very word *desires* brought with it the unexpected and most unwanted image of a roguish, devilishly handsome man, the sort who could tempt her to kick off her boots and run barefoot across the wide green lawn.

Glancing over her shoulder at the stairs, she wondered where Poppy might be—as well as Lord Halwell, who was driving down from London to fetch them.

It was beyond time for her to be gone from Owle Park and the unexpected memories it evoked. That, and the only souls left in the house were her, Poppy, the housekeeper, Mrs. Briar, and the woman's son.

And Mr. Muggins, Henrietta thought wryly, looking over at the dog, who was sitting up and looking toward the door.

As she looked up as well, the crunch of carriage wheels on the drive told her it was finally time to go.

Hen couldn't help herself. She sighed. Lord Halwell was

handsome enough, but hardly the sort to inspire dangerous, reckless desires.

Which was most excellent, she told herself. Yet again. Because from this day forth, she was going to remain steadfast, cool and reserved.

A respectable widow, above reproach.

As long as you avoid him, Poppy would tell her in her all too blunt fashion.

And by *him*, her outspoken maid did not mean Lord Halwell.

But *him*.

The first man to ever kiss Henrietta. The only man who had ever found his way into her heart. The one man she was supposed to despise and deplore above all others.

The one who tempted her like no other. Left her shivering with wonderment at the forbidden desires he could spark inside her by merely stepping into a room.

Hen shuddered and realized perhaps it was a most fortuitous bit of happenstance that Lord Halwell was here to save her from making some impetuous, colossal mistake. The sort of temptation that was all too close at hand here at Owle Park.

So she hurried to the door, ready to forget the past, only to find that her single most regrettable mistake was coming home to roost.

A ghost from her past, Poppy would point out.

An unexpected happening if ever there was one.

For the gentleman bounding down from the curricle wasn't the sunny and affable Lord Halwell but the glowering form of one Viscount Dale.

Or rather, *him.*

And the very sight of him whisked her back to the day they'd first met. The day she'd lost her heart.

Owle Park, nine years earlier

Lady Henrietta Seldon looked across the wide expanse of lawn toward the distant bit of woods and wondered if she dared. The dark green of the trees and the promise of shade and perhaps a bit of a breeze from the river beyond beckoned with the hint of respite from the day's heat.

And since she rarely got to spend such time in the country, she decided she did. Dare, that is.

For you see, as the daughter of a duke, there wasn't much that was allowed. At least not anything unchaperoned, and only then if she was well guarded and surrounded by the strictures and rules of Society.

Well, not today, she mused.

Hen, as the family called her, slipped out of the carriage, leaving behind her erstwhile chaperone of the moment, Great-Aunt Zillah, who was happily and most predictably snoring away. Hen nearly danced across the soft emerald green sea of grass, dropping her shawl and pelisse as she went. When she was far enough away from the carriage, she shed her boots and stockings so she could run barefoot, like a regular country lass.

Her hat, which she loved, what with its fetching, upturned brim and the jaunty plumes pinned there, she left on. Better than returning to London with her face tanned and freckled.

Her mother would be in horrors—especially with her impending presentation at Court and her debut ball.

Not that she truly needed either. She was all but promised to Lord Astbury—had been since they were young, but her mother was adamant that Hen have a proper Season in London.

However today she was going to have a bit of an adventure.

Patting her hat to make sure it was secure, she sighed with delight at the feel of the damp, cool grass beneath her feet. It was heaven—all of it. From the clean, crisp air, to the soft ground beneath one's feet, to the happy, teasing call of birds twittering overhead.

How her father and mother could prefer London to this blissful bucolic life, she would never understand.

As she glanced over her shoulder, a moment of sadness rushed over her. For as lovely as Owle Park was, it was a house clouded by tragedy. Her much older half brother, James, and nearly his entire family had died of a terrible fever in this house.

Closing her eyes, Hen struggled to recall the fleeting memories of her sibling who'd been the only issue of her father's first marriage. Memories of James were vague and mostly lost, but it was his children—who had been closer in age to her, since her father had remarried her mother at such a late age—their faces and voices she remembered more vividly. Kindly and beautiful Dove; tall and upright Freddie, the one who was to inherit; mischievous Felix with a twinkle in his eye that always promised trouble and great fun; and dear baby Lydia, who had just begun to walk—and on this very lawn.

All so beloved, and all of them swept away in a matter of days by a terrible fever.

Save Christopher, who was now her father's heir and would one day be the Duke of Preston.

Still, Papa could only bring himself to visit Owle Park but once a year—an annual inspection—and he never brought Christopher.

Turning from the house, Hen glanced again at the woods and recalled a path that Felix had shown her once. It led to a grand tree house the boys had built, and she wondered if it still stood.

There was only one way to find out.

She set off with a determined stride and very quickly found the narrow path, but the turns and shortcuts Felix had followed by rote eluded her memories, and all too quickly she was hopelessly lost in the thick trees and dense undergrowth.

"Dash my wig," she muttered under her breath, using one of Aunt Zillah's numerous colorful curses, for Hen knew only too well she was in the suds.

Oh, if only it was just the lost part. There was also the matter of *the line*.

And yes, that was exactly how a Seldon thought of it. In italics and if necessary, underlined several times.

<u>*The line*</u>.

The boundary that separated Owle Park from the neighboring estate, Langdale. Wherein lived the worst sort of devils.

The Dales.

Henrietta shuddered. Rogues, villains and devils, all of them.

Capable of ruining a gel with merely a glance, or so Aunt Zillah avowed.

How such a thing was possible, Hen was not interested in finding out.

So it was that when she heard the sharp bark of a dog, she nearly jumped out of her gown. For it brought to mind her old nanny's stories of Drogo Dale, who had allegedly hunted for wayward children with his pack of hellhounds and chased them still from his grave.

Even as she tried to tell herself that this dog might belong to someone who could point her in the right direction, she realized it wasn't just one hound's baying but the raucous cacophony of an entire pack.

A hellish one, she was certain. *Say, perhaps, Drogo's. . .*

This time she did curse, much as Aunt Zillah was prone to do, and turned to run, not caring about boundaries or lines or ruin, but with only one panicked thought: to be as far from these bloodthirsty fiends as her feet could carry her.

Yet as much as Hen loved the country, she was unused to wooded paths, and as she turned in her headlong flight, she failed to see the fallen tree and thorny bush behind her, over which she tumbled in a grand heap of muslin and lace, landing face-first in the soft dirt. Her knee smarted with the sting of a cut, her hands were definitely scraped, and for the life of her, she couldn't get up—her skirt having caught on one of the stubby dead branches and the tangle of thorns.

There was also the very humiliating realization that the cool breezes she'd sought in the woods were now blowing right up over her bare legs and, good heavens, her backside, which she had to imagine was in full view for all to see.

In fact, the only thing that had survived unscathed—that is after a hasty check—was her dear hat.

Small miracle that. And certainly no consolation when she was caught in a most indelicate position.

No, make that *ruinous*.

The mad hounds grew closer, and the more she tried to right herself, the more she found herself caught in the briars.

Literally.

Then all around her, the bushes crashed and the dogs descended upon her, circling her in a mad frenzy of barking—delighted to have found their prey.

"Oh, get away! Away with you!" she tried ordering, to no avail.

Then from behind her came a rich, deep voice. "Ho, there, you mad fools, what have you found?" This was followed by the solid *thud* of boots as they quickly and easily stalked through the woods.

Henrietta's panic stilled—though only for a second.

For one thing, it was hardly the voice of a ghost. And secondly, something about the man's languid tones nestled deeply into her sensibilities. It was a voice rich with aristocratic breeding and authority—a gentleman.

That alone was reassuring, but it was his delight at the very hint of some hereto-unknown discovery that caught her ear.

A curiosity she understood, for hadn't the very same desire to turn a corner led her here?

"Call them off! Please call off your dogs," she pleaded.

"Hup!" he barked, and all the dogs, to a one, sat on their haunches and stilled, having cleared the way for their master.

Henrietta was about to sigh with relief. That is, until she heard a low whistle of admiration. The humiliating sort coaching lads made at pretty girls. Or rowdies on a street corner might cast out to get a lady to look in their direction.

Whatever was he whistling about?

Then she remembered her skirt was up over her backside.

She closed her eyes and groaned. Good heavens, no!

"Oh, please don't come any closer," she called out. "I fear I'm not decent."

"Utterly divine would be a better description," her would-be rescuer teased.

Henrietta's cheeks flamed with heat. At least this rakish fellow couldn't see her embarrassment.

If that was any consolation.

She tried to reach around and tug her skirt down to some level of modesty, but it was good and caught, and when that didn't work, she tried to right herself again, only to become mired further.

"I do believe you are trapped, fair nymph," he pointed out.

"Yes, I am quite aware of that," she huffed, wishing she could see his face—if only to determine if he was a gentleman and not some rogue.

"I could help," he offered.

"Would you please?" she asked, feeling a moment of relief. Yes, he was a gentleman.

Though all-too-quickly his breeding came into question. "I think not," he replied.

"Whatever do you mean? You can't leave me like this."

"I suppose not, but helping you is hardly to my benefit," he explained, a devilish bit of humor behind his words.

Henrietta hardly shared in his amusement. "As a gentleman, you should have come to my aid immediately."

"What? And lose this vantage point?" She could almost hear him shake his head. "Why would I do that?"

Henrietta set her jaw and reminded herself she was the daughter of a duke, a lady in name and breeding, and that while she was being ogled by some ill-mannered ruffian who thought himself quite amusing—for now she was certain he was no gentleman—she must remain a lady.

Even if his behavior was insupportable.

Instead, she counted to ten.

One . . . two . . .

She'd grown up with Henry and Christopher—two rogues in their own right—and they'd teased her mercilessly over the years.

Three . . . four . . .

And yet . . . this was nothing less than an egregious effrontery.

Five . . . six . . .

Botheration, she fumed silently, then realized she'd lost count. And lost her patience.

"Get. Me. Up. Or so help me—" she ground out, forgetting all her vows to remain a lady.

"If you insist," he replied, all easy manners and teasing tones.

"I do."

As he came stalking closer, his pack of unruly mutts quivered with excitement, as if saying, *Look what we found!*

Hounds all of them. Dogs and master.

"You'll need to unhook my skirt," she told him, trying to point where she thought it was caught.

He chuckled. "Never had a lady offer so quickly."

"Oh!" Hen sputtered. "You are no gentleman!"

"The fact that I've merely glanced at your lovely limbs proves I am."

He'd merely glanced?! Of all the cheeky, wretched . . . she'd wager he'd done much more than "merely glanced."

Henrietta twisted to get a look at him, but out of the corner of her eye all she could spy was a dark, bottle green jacket and a long arm reaching toward her.

Dear heavens! Whatever did he intend to do? She couldn't help herself; she panicked a bit.

At her frantic movements, the dogs began their caterwauling yet again.

"Settle down, all of you," he told them with an authoritative snap.

Henrietta blanched as she realized he was including her in that order.

Of all the humiliating . . .

Once again, her rescuer whistled low and long. "You are good and trapped."

"Yes, well, if I hadn't been overrun by your pack of mongrels—"

"Mongrels?" He had the audacity to sound affronted. "I'll have you know my dogs are—"

"Ill-mannered, untrained—"

"They did find you," he pointed out.

Much to her chagrin and against everything she'd been raised to consider about a man, she found that his teasing made her blush as much as her predicament did. But she wasn't about to let him know this.

"*Harrumph*," she managed. After all, none of this was getting her upright and her skirt down where it belonged.

Covering her from prying eyes.

A fact he must also have understood, for here he was, laughing yet again. "Yes, well, let me get you untangled."

Then he did just that, catching hold of her ankle and starting to lift her foot.

His hand, warm and strong on her bare ankle, sent shock waves up Henrietta's limb and left her gasping for breath. Never had any man touched her so, and she certainly wasn't prepared for how intimate it was for someone—especially a stranger—to take such a liberty.

At the sound of her sharp intake of breath, he let go of her. "Did I hurt you? Are you injured?"

Something about the sincerity of his words washed away the bulk of her fears, and Henrietta felt more than a bit foolish. He was, after all, helping her, and to do that he had to touch her . . .

But more alarming was a very insensible desire trembling inside her that wanted very much to feel the warmth of his touch yet again.

"I don't want to hurt you," he continued to say.

"No, no," she rushed to tell him. "Just startled is all. Pray continue."

Because she didn't quite believe a single touch could truly send one's heart racing so . . .

Yet when he caught hold of her again, the heat of his touch left her breathless.

And yes, her heart went galloping along as if by a will of its own.

Gently he raised her foot and tugged at her skirt, and then again pulled at it, until fabric ripped—oh, it was a terrible shame, for she did love this muslin—and her gown came loose.

"There," he proclaimed as she felt the soft cotton fall down in place over her legs. "Now, are you certain you are unhurt?"

"Yes," she replied just as quietly.

Unhurt? Yes. But something was wrong with her heart.

For it was hammering about like a horse running wild.

"Then let me help you up." And with that, one strong hand caught hold of her wrist while another wound around her waist and he plucked her out of her tumbled state.

In an instant, Henrietta's world was both righted and tipped upside down.

Her hands came to rest on the only steady thing available—the man's chest—a solid wall of muscled strength. Catching hold of his lapels, she found her footing and looked up.

In the years that followed, she always wondered at what happened next.

Her breath failed her as her heart fell into an abyss.

Her rescuer, this supposed rogue, *was* indeed a gentleman. The most handsome one she'd ever seen. Golden brown hair fell loose from where it was tied in a country queue. He had a rugged jaw that was covered in rough stubble, but it was his eyes—blue as her mother's favorite sapphires—that caught her with their sparkle. They teased her with an impish spark that, as a Seldon, she knew only too well.

That light called to her every wild desire, her secret wishes. Ones, she had to imagine, she didn't yet understand.

And when he smiled, she knew without a doubt that one

day, this man, this ragged daring rogue, would show her the way.

Personally. Intimately.

In that instant, she wondered what it would be like to spend the rest of her life basking in his admiring gaze. To be the spark that illuminated such a passionate glow.

To her amazement, he seemed caught in the same spell, gazing down at her with a mixture of awe and amazement on his face, as if she were suddenly the nymph he'd called her earlier.

And she wasn't wrong about that.

"Well, I seem to have found my very own Calypso," he teased as he looked her up and down, reaching out to tuck a stray strand of her hair back up into her bonnet.

"I'm hardly—" she protested, trying at the same time to breathe.

Not that she had much of a chance to say anything more, not when he stopped her by putting a finger to her lips. "That and more."

Henrietta drew a steadying breath, undone by the magic that was his touch.

"How is it that you, O Goddess, came to be lost in my woods?" he said quietly, as if his words might frighten her to take flight into the nearest glen. His finger moved from her lips to curve under her chin and tip her head toward him, even as he dipped down closer to her.

Whatever am I supposed to do? Hen thought in a new sort of panic. He meant to kiss her.

Right here, right now. Oh, it was beyond ruinous.

Her heart did another of those galloping leaps of terror, for she'd never been kissed.

And worst of all? *She wanted him to.*

Very much so. Her hand rose up and her fingers touched the stubble on his jaw, grazing over the rough edges as she marveled at his ragged appearance.

She'd never seen a gentleman in such a state—a plain jacket, worn breeches, scuffed boots. In the world of London, he would be considered undressed. Unsuited. Alarmingly gauche.

Henrietta found him utterly desirable.

He smiled at her innocent exploration, caught her hand and held it to his cheek, even as he bent down to kiss her. His lips curved into a tantalizing smile, one of conquest won, and filled with the thrill of discovery.

She was his. That's what the wry curve of his lips said all too clearly.

His.

That single word sparked an altogether different awakening inside her. What had he said earlier?

His woods.

How could that be? The only property that abutted Owle Park belonged to . . .

Henrietta's mouth fell open. Which was probably both unsightly and definitely not the proper pose for a lady about to be kissed.

"*Your woods?*" she managed. "No, this is—" And then she stopped and looked at him again.

"Henrietta? Henrietta, where are you?" Her father's deep commanding voice rang through the trees.

This was followed by the estate steward's cry, "My lady? Lady Henrietta?"

The man before her stilled.

There they stood, his lips so very close to hers, his breath mingling over her as if in tantalizing whispers that had only added to her desire.

Then came that fateful question. "Who the devil are you?"

But they both knew the answer to that, even as Henrietta knew without a doubt who he was.

"No," she whispered. "Say it isn't true."

But it was. They both knew it, and he let go of her as if she suddenly burned, his features stricken.

"Henrietta Seldon! Where are you?" her father bellowed, his voice growing closer.

Not that it mattered, for Henrietta's entire world was this little glen, where she stood facing her rescuer, her Lancelot. Or, as it turned out, her very own Romeo.

For there it was, three hundred years of family animosity, a deep and binding feud that made them enemies, tore them apart before they'd even begun.

Her vision narrowed until it seemed the circle of trees around them had turned into a whirl and she was trapped in the middle.

Heaven's sake, her heart was. Turning, that is.

As the crash through the woods announced the impending arrival of her father, the man before her bowed and went to the edge of the glen.

There he paused and took one last look at her. "Go, my little Calypso," he whispered, nodding in the direction of her father. And then he turned briskly, snapped his fingers and stalked into the woods, his dogs following in unison, silently, as if they too felt their master's grief.

When he got nearly out of sight, he turned once more and took one last look at her. Longing and desire filled his eyes, but the set of his jaw told the true story.

There were some lines that couldn't be crossed.

And that very image of Crispin, Viscount Dale—handsome and rugged, steely and determined—Henrietta Seldon carried in her heart until the next time they met.

Chapter Two

Every Dale is given the same
middle name: Obstinate.

A Seldon family adage

Owle Park, 1810

"I've come to see Preston," Viscount Dale told Henrietta as he came marching up the steps, his announcement, or rather demand, wrenching her back to the present.

Well, of all the arrogant, presumptuous . . .

"He's not here. He and the duchess have returned to London. Seek him there," she told him, turning on one heel and about to slam the door in his face, but he was too quick for her, having wedged his boot in the doorjamb and then easily shouldering it open, striding in like the conquering hero.

She pointed toward the drive. "Get out or I'll have you tossed out."

An idle threat if ever there was one.

There was only Mrs. Briar and her son in the house. And dear Mrs. Briar was deaf as a post, while her son was a kindly, simple boy who was perfect for fetching horses and carrying in more kindling, but hardly the type to toss this devil of a rogue out by his well-appointed breeches.

Nor was Tabitha's renowned dog much help. Mr. Muggins sat beside her and watched the viscount through narrowed eyes.

Henrietta hoped that meant the dog was about to make good his wretched reputation and chase this villain from the premises.

But not even that was meant to be, as Mr. Muggins just held his position.

For his part, Lord Dale hardly seemed to care that the object of his quest wasn't available. He turned his sharp, blue-eyed gaze on Henrietta, and she nearly shivered.

Because it was when Crispin Dale looked at her thusly that mayhem usually ensued.

Mayhem of the heart.

The worst sort, in her estimation.

"Get out," she told him, pointing again at the door. *Before you wreak havoc on my life. Yet again.*

Words she wouldn't give him the satisfaction of hearing.

"You'll do," he told her, setting down a large hamper before her.

At this, Mr. Muggins sat up, softly whimpering, then coming over to nudge the lid of the large basket.

"Yes, you hell-bound mongrel, your sins have finally come home to roost," Crispin told the dog.

"Whatever are you talking about?" Henrietta demanded. "What is the meaning of all this?"

"The meaning?" he sputtered, then reached over and flipped open the lid.

There was a brief second when Henrietta realized exactly what was inside the basket, before the contents erupted in a whimpering, barking melee of puppies.

"That . . . that beast," he told her, pointing at Mr. Muggins, "got my best hunting bitch pregnant."

So there it was. History repeating itself. Wasn't this how the entire feud had begun all those centuries ago? Over an ill-begotten litter.

A litter of prized hunting pups intended as a gift for Queen Elizabeth—set to have been born when Her Majesty had been due to arrive at Langdale during one of her summer progresses. Save the puppies had come out looking exactly like one of the Duke of Preston's infamous mongrels.

Oh, how the queen and the duke—one of her favorites—had laughed over it, but the Dales had never forgotten the humiliation.

So here was Crispin, glaring at her as if she had sent Mr. Muggins over with just that intent.

To impugn their reputation once again.

Well, he could glare all he wanted. Henrietta wasn't a Seldon for nothing. She scowled right back at him.

After all, hadn't Crispin's cousin, that vixen Daphne Dale, recently seduced Henrietta's own dear brother, Henry—sensible and responsible Henry—into a scandalous runaway marriage, reopening all the old wounds between the two clans?

These pups, as far as she was concerned, were just desserts.

"Well?!" Crispin demanded.

Henrietta glanced again at the pups and then at Mr. Muggins. Oh, there was no denying that these pups were his—same rough coat, same wild manners—but she was feeling mulish.

"However do you know that Mr. Muggins is responsible?" she asked, even when her eyes told her quite clearly that the basket full of scruffy mongrels could come from only one source.

Without missing a beat, Lord Dale reached inside his jacket and drew out what, she supposed, had once been part of a feather-trimmed glove. He held it over that basket, and in unison all seven puppies began to growl.

As did Mr. Muggins.

That is until she shot the big oaf of a dog a dark glance.

"Well, yes, I suppose they might be of the same breed," she conceded.

"A breed indeed! As if I would expect a Seldon to know anything about good breeding," he said, sparing a glance at Mr. Muggins. "But that isn't my problem. Not any longer."

He began to leave, and good riddance, she thought—until, that is, she realized what he intended.

"You can't think to leave those . . . those . . ."

"Mongrels?" he offered.

"Puppies," she corrected, if only not to offend Mr. Muggins—she had her plumed hat to think of. "You cannot leave them with me. Whatever am I to do with seven puppies?"

She shot another aggrieved glance at Mr. Muggins.

Leave it to an Irish terrier to be so prolific.

"Take them to Preston, with my compliments," Lord Dale replied as he continued toward the door.

"Oh, no! Don't you dare! This is—" Hen began, until, that is, one of the puppies jumped out of the hamper and began scampering around the foyer. Inspired by their sibling's new-found freedom, the others followed suit, bounding this way and that, and Hen scrambled to gather them up.

For his part, Viscount Dale just stood in the middle of the mayhem, arms crossed, still looking as if his entire family had been besmirched.

"Oh, bother, don't just stand there," Henrietta snapped. "Help me." Glancing over her shoulder, she spied one of the pups venturing down the steps into the wine cellar.

Good heavens, she'd forgotten to close the door.

Down the steps the puppy went, and Henrietta followed into the darkness. And got halfway down before she realized she'd need some light to find the little fellow.

"Crispin, I'll break my neck in the dark down here," she called out. "Bring down the candle."

She heard him muttering about "always having to come to your aid," but she ignored his complaint once he appeared at the top of the steps and followed her down into the dark of the cellar.

Mrs. Briar came bustling out into the foyer and blundered to a stop at the sight before her, even as her son, Charlie, came up the front steps.

"Oh, goodness," she exclaimed, pointing at one of the pups, "catch hold of that one before it gets out."

Charlie caught the little scamp, and together they quickly had the entire pack corralled back in the hamper.

Hands fisted to her hips, Mrs. Briar took only one glance at the pups and then Mr. Muggins to put two and two together. "Made yourself at home in the neighborhood, did you?" she said with a laugh, gathering up the basket. Spying the carriage in the drive, and her ladyship's valise sitting abandoned near the door, she didn't need any explanation as to what had happened when Lord Halwell had arrived.

Well, the lady was a widow. Three times over. And Mrs. Briar wasn't one to comment on the goings-on of her betters, even if she did sniff a bit with disapproval.

Instead, she instructed Charlie to drive the carriage down to the stables. "Must be that Lord Halwell Her Ladyship said was due to arrive." She glanced up the stairs and decided not to go seeking out Lady Juniper until the lady summoned her.

"Bad as you," she told Mr. Muggins, then turned to take the pups down to the kitchen. And when she did, she noticed that the door to the wine cellar was wide open.

"That won't do," she muttered and promptly shut the door, throwing the latch shut. "Won't have anyone blaming me for the wine going missing." She huffed a sigh. "Come on, you little mites. I think I have some nice milk just in."

And she toddled off to the kitchen, Mr. Muggins following behind her, sparing the door to the wine cellar one last knowing, well-pleased glance.

"Oh, here he is," Henrietta called out from the back of the cellar. "However did you get so far afield so quickly?"

Even as she said the words, she heard the door to the wine cellar close with a decided thud.

"No!" she gasped, pushing past Crispin and dashing for the stairs. When she reached the door she pushed at it, but it was as she feared: locked tight.

"Mrs. Briar! Mrs. Briar! Please, open the door!"

But there was no reply. Good heavens, she was trapped.

It was then she remembered who else shared her predicament.

Him.

That was when Henrietta truly panicked.

"You might as well stop," Henrietta told Crispin after he spent the next hour pounding on the door. "As I've said before, Mrs. Briar is nearly deaf—she won't hear you unless she is right next to the door."

"I'm not willing to give up just yet. We Dales don't abandon ship at the first leak."

The words rattled Hen. For now he wasn't talking about the door or their current plight. He was slighting her.

"I never—" she began and stopped just as quickly. Especially when one of his brows quirked up.

Well, perhaps she had given up. Once. Or twice. But in her heart she'd never been able to stop her feelings for him. And besides, each time she'd been quite certain it was Crispin who had "abandoned ship."

"And if I hadn't 'given up,' then what, Lord Dale? Would you have declared your undying love for me? A Seldon?" She snorted and settled back down on the stool she'd claimed.

Beside her, the errant pup, the one who had led them down into this dungeon of sorts, slept in a crate she'd found for it. "Would you have married me? Invited your dear Aunt Damaris to the wedding?"

When Crispin didn't respond, she huffed again and crossed her arms over her chest. "So I thought."

After a few moments, he stomped down the steps and sat down on the last one, his long legs stuck out in front of him. "I gave you my word," he repeated stubbornly.

Obstinately. So very much like a Dale.

She stole a glance at him.

Those words, that promise, were exactly why everything had gone so very wrong.

Chapter Three

Once bewitched by a Seldon beauty,
madness is your only salvation.

A WARNING GIVEN TO ALL DALE
MALES FROM THE TIME THEY
ARE IN SHORT PANTS

London, 1802

A grand masked ball was the sort of thing a Seldon loved,
and the Duke of Preston's masquerade in honor of his daughter's presentation at Court was no exception.

Every important family in the *ton* had been invited, which
was to say, they all were.

Save one. But no one ever mentioned them in front of the
duke.

Not if they wanted an invitation to the next fête or soirée.

Nor had Hen noticed. With such a grand crush, a full
dance card and free-flowing champagne, Henrietta had been
too busy dancing every dance. Now with it well after mid-

night, she wasn't paying attention as she ought to her choice of companion.

"Who are you supposed to be?" Lord Bertram asked, his breath awash with brandy. He was the third son of a marquess, and she had agreed to dance with him only because their mothers were friends—that, and as a child, Bertie had often been brought to the Seldon nursery to play with Christopher and Henry.

Though he, like her brother and nephew, had learned quickly that she ruled the roost above stairs.

"Some sort of goddess or the like?" Bertie guessed after another leering glance at her costume.

"Calypso," Hen supplied.

He snorted. "Ah, yes. She's a bit of a wanton, now, isn't she?" He leaned over and tugged her rather close, his brows waggling at her in what he probably assumed was a seductive air.

It wasn't. Hen's stomach rolled.

"It is merely a costume," she told him, trying to get a bit of distance between them, but unfortunately, Bertie had her in his clutches and was steering her out the garden doors.

"*Wan-n-n-ton*," he repeated, his drink-addled tongue slurring the word. "I rather like that about you, Henny. All grown up and filled out nicely"—he took another leering glance at her breasts—"but I can't see why you're thinking of wasting all that on such a dull stick as Astbury. Now with me, I'd give you something you'd never be bored with."

His full, wet lips came dipping down toward her, and she twisted her head away, desperate to escape his grasp. "Bertie, let go of me this instant."

But her undisputed authority from the schoolroom no longer held sway in this milieu, and Bertie was determined, since he presumed he now had the upper hand.

Though as it turned out, the smug lordling wasn't the only one about.

"Unhand the lady," a firm, deep voice commanded.

"Eh?" Bertie muttered, glancing over his shoulder. "Shove off. I was here first."

"And now I'm here. Leave."

Henrietta looked up—for there was something very familiar about this man's voice. And when she spied his costume, saw the burnished gold of his hair and the piercing blue of his eyes behind his mask, her heart nearly leapt from her chest. "Odysseus," she gasped.

No. It couldn't be. He wouldn't dare.

And yet it was him.

Him. That was how she'd thought of him since they'd met in the woods at Owle Park. *Him.*

Better that than by his real name.

Viscount Dale. Or rather Crispin, as she'd learned from a secretive foray through her mother's volume of *Debrett's.*

Yes, Crispin.

The man who had stopped and started her heart. The rogue who'd been about to kiss her.

And that time she'd wanted to be kissed.

Still did. By him, that is.

"I said, leave the lady alone," Crispin repeated.

"And I said shove off," Bertie replied, this time with a rude hand gesture.

Crispin moved in a blur—fast and furious—using every

bit of muscle he had, all earned in a rigorous country life.

Solid, unforgiving strength Hen remembered from when her fingers had fanned out over his chest.

The viscount had Bertie in his grasp in an instant, and now the third son of a marquess was nothing more than a puppet in his hands, dangling in the air. "Listen well," Crispin told him in a voice black with anger, "this lady is off limits to you. Forever."

"Now see here—" Bertie had the audacity to demand, that is until Crispin gave him a good shake, like a hunting dog with a rodent.

The viscount hauled Bertie closer so they were eye to eye, and his voice was level and sure. "You will leave now or you will leave with a black eye and a broken nose." Then he gave him another rattle for good measure and tossed him aside.

Bertie barely managed to land on his feet, and he scurried away like the loathsome little rat that he was.

After making sure the fellow was well and gone, Crispin turned to her. "He didn't harm you, did he?"

"Who? Bertie?" Hen shook her head, still a little bit dazed.

At her rescue.

At his arrival back in her life.

She glanced back at the ballroom. "Bertie's always been a bit of a cur. But I had things well in hand." She did her best to still her trembling hands by smoothing at the creases in her gown.

Crispin laughed. "Did you now?"

"Well, perhaps not," she admitted, glancing up at him and smiling slightly. "Thank you for rescuing me."

"*Again*," he teased. "You do find yourself in predicaments, don't you, my dear Calypso?"

"I suppose. But perhaps that is why you are my Odysseus." Hen glanced shyly up at him and was struck that it hadn't been just her imagination—Crispin Dale was terribly and wickedly handsome.

Crispin Dale. Of all people! Why did it have to be him?

And then a second thought occurred to her. What the devil was he doing here? A Dale inside a Seldon house. Why, it was not to be borne!

And she knew what she should say. *Get out.*

But those words lodged in her throat. Instead, she asked the one question she truly wanted to know. "What are you doing here?"

"You stole my heart, Calypso. I merely came to get it back."

Beyond them, the open doors of the ballroom sent a shaft of light into the garden. She spied her brother walking past the opening and realized just how precarious her situation was. Far more than it had ever been with Bertie.

"You shouldn't be here," she told Crispin, pulling him deeper into the shadows of the garden.

"My Aunt Damaris is right—you Seldons are licentious creatures at heart. Trying to bewitch me, are you?"

She took a step back from him, putting the graveled path between them. "Whyever would you say that?"

"The first time we met, you asked me to unhook your skirt, and now you've maneuvered me out here—alone—into the scandalous reaches of your gardens. Perhaps when you are done seducing me, fair Calypso, you could show me where your father and his Hell Fire club meet."

She crossed her arms over her chest. "Oh, of all the ridiculous notions. My father is happily married to my mother. Hell Fire club indeed!"

He grinned at her. "If you insist—"

"I do—"

"You can't be angry with me," he told her, stepping into the middle of the path, erasing the line between them. "After all, I rescued you."

"From Bertie," she pointed out, as if that made his heroics hardly worth mentioning. "And perhaps I've brought you here because it will be easier to push you out the gate." She tipped her head toward the heavy wooden portal that led to the mews.

"And yet you haven't," he said, reaching out to take her hand in his. "I think I know why you led me here."

"You do?" she managed as he pulled her closer.

"Yes," he murmured, "to gain that kiss you tried to steal from me back in my woods."

"Those woods are ours," she told him, a state of delicious wonder enveloping her. She only hoped he didn't notice she didn't deny the first part.

That she wanted him to kiss her.

She did, heaven help her. She'd spent all these months since they'd last met wondering, daydreaming, of what might have happened between them if her father hadn't happened along when he had. Months spent delirious with curiosity, an unending desire to know what that moment would be like when his lips brushed against hers.

He leaned closer so his breath whispered over the curve of her ear. "I came tonight to give you your heart's desire—"

Well, of all the arrogant, presumptuous, wonderful . . .

". . . and to say good-bye."

He pulled her close and dipped his head down to claim exactly what he sought: her lips.

Henrietta reeled back. "Good-bye? Whatever for?"

"I'm leaving, fair Calypso. With the peace treaty all signed, I am off to Paris. Morning after next, in fact."

"Paris?" But it was another notion that hammered at her heart. *So soon?*

"Yes. To Paris and Italy and all the sights in between." His lips brushed against the lobe of her ear, his breath teasing over her bare neck.

Henrietta shivered, for his touch was filled with promise . . . and possibilities. As difficult as it was to think, and as beguiling as he was, Henrietta drew back, for it was his words that caught her imagination. "Paris? And Italy?"

She sighed with an entirely different longing. Oh, how could a single word be so seductive?

Paris.

And to her amazement, he understood her longing. "I sail down the Thames morning after next. Then across the Channel. I'll be in Paris in a week."

Envy filled her. "Oh, that sounds so wondrous. I've never sailed anywhere." When she'd suggested as much to Astbury for a possible wedding trip, he'd shuddered at the notion.

Crispin, on the other hand, seemed to share her excitement. "I imagine it will be cramped and smell like fish. The crossing, that is. But then again, what is a little discomfort when I will be in France at the end of it."

"Oh, yes," Hen agreed, waving off any such inconveniences.

"And then you'll have all of Europe at your beck and call." She couldn't help herself—she made a little pirouette before him, unable to contain her own excitement.

"I suppose," he laughed.

She came to a stop and caught hold of his sleeve. "And the Tuileries, will you go there?"

"How could I not?" He retook her hand, as if promising.

"You must write me and tell me of everything," she instructed, ignoring how her family would react to her receiving missives from a Dale. "I want to hear all about the paintings, and the gardens. And the shops. And of course, the fashions."

Before he could add another word, she rushed to continue, "And will you sit in one of the cafes in Paris and sip coffee?"

"I believe that is most definitely on the agenda," he told her.

"Was watching the wicked ladies stroll by also on that agenda?" she teased back.

"No, never," he told her in mock horror, but the roguish light in his eyes said otherwise.

"Well, read them poetry," she advised. Then quickly changed her mind. "No, please don't. I'd prefer it if you didn't."

He laughed again. "No wicked ladies. I will strike them from my list. Save the one from home who holds my heart."

She opened her mouth to protest, then realized he meant her. She knew she should correct him, but she found instead she rather liked that he thought her quite wicked.

And that she held his heart. It was a starry, magical moment that left her a bit off kilter.

"Oh, how I would love to see all those things," she told

him, rushing past her disorientation. "And if you are in Paris, you must go to—" Then she stopped, remembering herself. "Heavens, I fear I am organizing you. Henry, my brother, and Christopher are forever telling me it is unbecoming in a lady."

"No, no," he told her, picking up a stray strand of her hair and tucking it behind her ear, his fingers grazing over her lobe, sending those agonizing tendrils of desire back through her yet again. "My aunt is rather against me going—me being the Dale, and not overly fond of my cousin who would inherit if anything—"

Harriet put her finger to his lips to stop him. "Don't say such a thing. 'Tis bad luck." Then conscious of what she was doing, she drew back her hand. "Yes, well, my father went on his tour all alone, and I've read his journals and seen his sketches, and I can't see how you will have anything but the most marvelous adventures. Will you go over the Alps like—"

And together they finished the sentence.

"Hannibal."

"Without the elephants," he confided as if disappointed, and they both laughed.

Their dreams, it seemed, were as entangled as their hearts.

Suddenly she felt a bit shy and at a loss what to do—for with him gone . . .

"If you leave—" she began.

"Never fear, fair Calypso, I shall return. For you. You have only to wait for me."

Before she could sputter a reply, because truly it was nothing but arrogance on his part to think she'd wait for him, he kissed her.

And the touch of his lips was like nothing she could have imagined. And it explained why he could so arrogantly ask her to do the impossible.

Wait for him.

Crispin showed her exactly what he meant.

Wait for me.

His lips brushed over hers, and like the moment she'd first looked into his eyes, his world tilted.

No, upended.

He'd come tonight to prove to himself he'd imagined their magical meeting in the woods. That the fair Calypso of his dreams couldn't possibly exist.

And yet, here she was. Her lips warm and sweet beneath his. She tried to back away, but he wound his arm around her waist and tucked her close until they were right up against each other.

His lips nudged at hers, opening her up, and his tongue ran over the slight opening he'd prompted from her.

And she returned his kiss exactly as he'd imagined, bold and passionate, bringing a sort of delirium with it.

His kiss deepened, and his hand cradled at her backside, bringing her right up against him.

All of him.

She let out a small mew of shock and . . . desire.

He knew all the stories about Seldon women—beguiling, bewitching creatures sent from the old gods to drive the usually staid and steady Dales mad.

Darius Dale, who'd been tempted by Celeste Seldon and

had left his vicarage in the middle of the night, never to be seen again.

Or Phineas Dale, who'd been about to marry his true love but had abandoned her at the altar to run away with a Seldon vixen, who'd similarly abandoned him.

Neither of them had heeded the warnings, and look how they'd ended up.

Mad. Lost. Abandoned.

Utter nonsense, Crispin had told himself over the years. Until now.

Certainly he could have satisfied his curiosity by observing Lady Henrietta in the park, or while she'd shopped, all from a safe distance, but instead he'd been drawn to deliberately breach that sacred line that divided the Seldons from the Dales. He'd snuck like a thief into the very bowels of his enemies for no other reason than the fact that he'd felt compelled.

Lured.

Yet here, on this very night, he'd convinced himself he could confront her and she wouldn't bolt free. Disappear into some sylvan glen and never be seen again. His goddess. His own Calypso.

So it hadn't been much of a surprise when he'd looked into her eyes and realized Henrietta was the most wild, tempestuous creature he'd ever beheld. And he knew, just knew down to his bones, that she might never be truly caught or tamed.

Just as every Dale prophecy about Seldon females warned.

Oh, Henrietta Seldon was the direct path to madness. Utter madness, he told himself. And yet, he couldn't let her go.

For so many reasons. The way her eyes had lit at the mention of Paris. Of crossing the Channel. Of climbing over Hannibal's Alps.

She shared his desires, his fantasies, and he wanted nothing more than to discover them with her at his side.

In coming here tonight, he'd answered all his doubts and discovered the truth. By seeing her, holding her, kissing her, it all became so clear.

To hell with waiting—risking that she'd come to her senses and remember that he was a Dale and she was a Seldon.

He'd ask her the impossible.

Pulling his lips away from hers, impetuously, recklessly, he offered her his heart.

"Come with me, Calypso. Come with me to Paris."

Henrietta was lost. Lost in a world she'd never imagined. No book could describe. Hot and languid desire coursed through her veins. Heated and anxious passion tugged in other parts.

Good heavens, how could he kiss her lips, stroke her bare shoulders and leave that spot between her legs clenched, tight and growing heated with every touch?

"Crispin," she murmured as his lips nibbled just behind her earlobe.

If he heard her, he made no note, only went back to the same spot and bedeviled it some more, as if called by a siren.

By her song.

Oh, if anyone was being called, it was her. Lured and lulled.

She'd never understood how it was that sensible, smart

young ladies could be led astray by some rogue . . . but now she knew.

Intimately so. Especially as his hand came up to cradle one of her breasts, his fingers teasing over the nipple . . .

Henrietta gasped, for his touch sent sparks of desire racing down her spine, cutting a rift through her, like a log cracked in half by the heat of the fire. And she knew she'd follow him anywhere if only he'd . . .

Then, as if by magic, he did just that.

He called to her.

"Come with me, Calypso," he whispered to her. "Come with me to Paris."

Come with him? How could he suggest such a thing?

However could she say no?

Especially when his fingers teased over her again, full of promise, and she saw the world—his world—the two of them in Paris, dancing in some elegant salon. Climbing over the ragged peaks and down into the beauty of Italy. Riding a gondola in Venice. Gazing upon the ancient ruins of Rome. Walking the streets of Verona like Romeo and Juliet might have.

Well, perhaps that isn't the best example, she mused.

But still, Hen was certain of one thing: Every night would be like this.

Full of promise and desires answered.

"Come with me," he whispered again.

Henrietta's thoughts swirled and she tried desperately to find some steady bit of reasoning—the sort Aunt Zillah claimed was lost on the young.

Here Hen had always thought of herself as quite sensible—that is, until now.

For she wanted nothing more than to dash out the back gate with Crispin Dale in tow and never look back.

How could she be sensible with his hard chest pressed to her breasts, his strong arms wound around her, his warm, steady hands exploring her with the surety of the most devilish rogue?

Oh, good heavens, she was lost . . . ever so . . .

That is until she heard her name from the most familiar voice she knew.

"Hen! Where the devil are you?"

Without even thinking, she stepped out of Crispin's warm embrace as if yanked by an invisible chain. Spinning around, she spied Henry standing in stark outline at the open doors.

When she glanced back at Crispin, she said in explanation, "My brother."

The rogue's brows rose, not so much in alarm at being caught seducing Lord Henry Seldon's sister but at the challenge of it.

Hen nearly groaned. *Men!*

However, Crispin's air of conquest vanished a bit when a second voice was added to Henry's.

Christopher appeared beside her brother. "Hen? Hen, if you are out here, Her Grace says she'll cancel your account at Madame Barousse's."

"Not my hats," she muttered in dismay.

"I'll buy you a trunk full in Paris," Crispin teased.

Henrietta covered her mouth to keep from laughing. The horrid rogue! He did know the way to a lady's heart.

Straight through a good milliner.

Henry and Christopher strode into the darkness of the

gardens. Christopher joked with her brother, "With her account closed, you know demmed well she'll wheedle the coins out of us."

"She can try," Henry replied.

"Ha! You know how she is. She'll tell Grandfather about that bit of mischief you ran into last month at that gaming hell, and you'll have no choice but to pay her bills."

"Oh, demmit. She would," Henry groused back. "Even when she knows I'll never make that mistake again."

Christopher chuckled. "Told you not to follow me."

As had Hen. But had Henry listened? No!

She couldn't help smiling—they both knew her so well—but then again, they had been raised together after Christopher's family had been lost, and there was only six months' difference between their ages, regardless of the fact that on the family tree she held the position of Christopher's aunt.

They had come further into the garden, close to where she and Crispin were hidden behind the arbor.

"She'll be Astbury's problem soon enough," Henry said.

"Heaven help the poor fellow," Christopher replied, glancing over his shoulder at the ballroom. "Does he have an inkling of what he's getting himself mired into?"

"Astbury?" Henry shook his head. "Poor fool is as besotted as the rest of the males in London. Demmed inconvenient to have such a fetching sister."

"Isn't it?" Christopher agreed. "Who'd have thought our Henhouse would grow into those ears?"

They both laughed, and Hen resisted the urge to box both of theirs. Ears, that is. And that horrible nickname. Her hands immediately balled into two tight fists.

They'd spent years teasing her that she had enormously large ears, as big as a henhouse, when it hadn't been the truth. Not in the least. But there it was, they had teased her nonetheless.

Henry finished up chortling and added, "You wouldn't believe the pups and lordlings who've pestered me of late for an introduction. Even Juniper came up. Steady, reliable Juniper, of all people!"

"No!" Christopher replied, clearly horrified. "Not Gusty!"

"Oh, yes, even Gusty. Muttering something about a decent introduction and putting in a good word for him." Her brother sighed. "Thought he was smarter than all that. But there it is— the most steady fellow ever, unflappable as they come, and Juniper has fallen like the rest. Not that it matters much when she's destined for Astbury."

And in unison the pair of them said with a laugh, "Poor sod."

Behind her, Crispin straightened. "Astbury?"

Hen winced, then glanced over her shoulder at him. "We are . . . well, not officially. It has just always been assumed. At least it was until—"

Until I met you, she wanted to add, but already there was a burning bit of anger in his expression.

"You're engaged?"

"No—it is just assumed—" When she saw that her rambling explanation was getting nowhere, she tried again. "It is hoped for. But that was before—" Oh, bother, however could she explain this?

And then it occurred to her there were no words.

She laid her hand on his heart, where beneath his jacket she could feel its steady beat. And when she looked up at him, she realized she didn't need to say anything.

He knew. "To Paris?"

Hen nodded. "To Paris."

Then a large, looming shadow passed over them.

"What is this, Hen?" Henry asked.

Hen snatched back her hand like a guilty child. Oh, heavens, now it all looked worse. So she drew a deep breath, turned around and, as regally as her mother might, gazed serenely at her brother and nephew, who stood before her shoulder to shoulder.

A wall of male suspicion.

"Nothing," she told him. "Actually, this gentleman came to my aid—rescued me from one of our more persistent guests."

"Who was that?" Christopher asked, suddenly sounding like a future duke. For it wasn't so much a question but a demand.

Not that she was about to tell them about Bertie. Tattling on that rat-faced little weasel had only ever gotten the three of them into trouble as children, and she didn't think they would fare any better now.

She looked from one to the other. "Mr. Dishforth."

Henry and Christopher exchanged a wary glance. For they both knew Dishforth—their imaginary foe from childhood, upon whom they always blamed their mistakes.

And it was also their own secret, immutable code for "none of your business."

With Dishforth therefore evoked, they were bound to inquire no further. However, that didn't stop them from turning their steely gazes on her companion.

"And so you brought Lady Henrietta out here, Lord—?" Christopher asked him, looking Crispin right in the eye.

Oh, dear heavens, what if either of them recognized who this was? Well, Hen didn't want to think about what would happen.

Yet as it turned out, Crispin was up to the challenge. "Only to allow her ladyship a moment of fresh air."

"—to settle my nerves," she added.

Which only served to make Henry and Christopher glower more. They both knew she gave nervous tremors, and most certainly never had them.

"Seems to be more than that," Henry replied in a low, menacing voice.

"No, not at all," Crispin replied smoothly, with a slight tip of his head. "I was leaving by the back gate—"

"Going so soon?" Christopher asked.

Crispin nodded amiably. "I'm off to Paris, day after next. Much to get in order." He smiled as if he hadn't heard any of Christopher's doubts. "As I was saying, when I spied Lady Henrietta in some distress, I came to her aid, and that is all."

"I owe this man a terrible debt," Hen told them both. Insisted, was more like it.

Henry crossed his arms over his chest, his jaw set in a hard line. "I suspect it has been repaid."

"Really!" she snapped. "How can you be so stodgy and rude, Henry? This man was kind enough to rescue me."

From a loveless marriage . . . from a life devoid of passion. . .

"But now I seem to be keeping you." Crispin bowed elegantly to Hen. "Good-bye, fair Calypso," he whispered for her and her alone.

"Safe travels, my lord," she said, holding out her hand for him.

His fingers curled around hers, and when they touched, that spark, that recognition lit between them.

Her gaze swung up, as did his, and it met, just as their hands had, with the wrenching understanding that if they let go, if they walked away now, the real casualty would be their hearts.

He leaned in and whispered softly, "Meet me at that gate just before dawn."

She didn't even have time to nod her assent, for then her father came to the doorway. "Ah, good, you've found her. Well done, lads. Come, Henrietta, your mother wishes to introduce you to Lady Jersey."

And there it was. The ducal command.

Henrietta stilled, for she'd never once disobeyed her father.

Not in a way that would leave her cut off from everything she knew and loved.

What small bit of practicality she did possess—an inheritance from her mother's side of the family, for goodness knows, no one had ever called a Seldon practical—reassured her there was a lifetime ahead of her to make amends for what she'd just agreed to do.

Time enough to convince her family that a union with a Dale, at least this one, wasn't the end of the world as they knew it.

At least so she believed as she turned to him and said once
again, "Safe travels, my lord. I hope I shall see you again very
soon."

O n the appointed morning, or rather, just before dawn,
Henrietta stole silently down the staircase of her father's
ducal town house.

She'd packed her own valise, donned her favorite blue hat,
and was ready for her grand adventure. With him.

Him.

No, she had to stop thinking of him as that. He was
Crispin Dale. Viscount Dale.

She cringed just slightly. Habit, she supposed. It was
rather hard to shake three hundred years of family animosity
with just a kiss.

But what a kiss, she thought dreamily as she paused at the
bottom step.

Gathering up her courage, she continued on, quietly
opening the door to the ballroom. From there it was simply
through the French doors to the garden and then . . . and
then . . .

Into Crispin's arms and off to Paris.

It was too much to believe. She grinned from ear to ear
and took two steps into the empty ballroom.

"Thought you'd go without saying good-bye?"

Henrietta whirled around.

Christopher!

Lounging in one of the chairs pushed up against the wall,
he smiled indolently at her.

"Where are you going?" he asked, rising from his post. "Paris?"

She flinched. "How the devil—?"

"Yes, well, my hearing is better than my morals. And since my morals aren't the best, I could tell that rogue you were with in the gardens the other night wasn't the rescuing type—"

"He's no rogue—"

"Yet he asks you to meet him at the gates at dawn?" He shrugged as if he could see no other conclusion, and for a moment she thought—well, could almost believe—that he was here to help her.

That is until his brows drew into a dark, unforgiving line.

Oh, bother. "Christopher, this is none of your affair," she told him, marching toward the doors as if she'd merely been going out to pick a few roses.

"I'll not let you leave, Hen. Not like this."

She stilled and glanced over her shoulder at him. Christopher! Of all people! He was on the road to being the most rakish Seldon ever, and he thought to lecture her?

"I am going," she replied and continued toward the door.

But by the time she got to it, her fingers winding around the latch, Christopher was there, his hand over her shoulder, holding the door shut. Tight.

"I owe Grandfather everything," he told her as she stood there with her back to him, shaking with anger. "I won't see His, or Her Grace's, heart broken over some ill-fated elopement."

She turned around and faced him, and something of her concerns must have shown in her eyes.

"Good God, Hen, this bounder did promise to marry you, didn't he?"

This took her aback, for even as she quickly recalled their conversation, she realized that Crispin's offer had never once mentioned marriage.

And her frantic realization was apparently obvious to her suddenly chivalrous nephew.

"Gads! What are you thinking?" Christopher nearly exploded. Then remembering the need for stealth, he lowered his voice. "Who is he?"

Hen shook her head, her jaw set as stubbornly as he'd set his. "I won't say. It is none of your business."

"Anything that brings shame upon this family or hurts Grandfather is my business."

Oh, this was a fine time for him to find his moral fortitude. Where had it been when he'd hauled Henry down to that Seven Dials stew last month?

"Stand aside," she told him, for even now she could see the first hints of dawn starting to rise in the sky beyond. Crispin had told her to be there before dawn, and the time was nearly past.

"No," he told her. And then without further word, he caught her around the middle and slung her over his shoulder like a sack of onions, carting her through the house further and further from the back gate.

Of all the indignities! Hen kicked and pounded on him, but Christopher just ignored her, knowing full well she couldn't cry out.

Not without bringing down the entire household to witness this scene. And worse, demand an explanation.

Then it occurred to her that all she had to do was go along with him. Then, once he was lured into believing she wasn't going to bolt out the door, she'd slip past him.

Certainly she could get to the docks before Crispin's boat sailed.

She just must!

But Christopher hadn't lived with her for all these years without being used to her tricks. The moment she stopped kicking up a fuss, he laughed.

"Won't work, Hen. I cannot allow you to do this." And without another word, he deposited her into the footman's closet in the front hall, closed the door in her face and locked it. She heard the distinctive scrape of a chair, and then what she assumed was Christopher settling in to wait her out.

She whirled around to find there was only the small oriel window in the corner, not even big enough for her to get her head out. And through the round window came the gleaming light that told the entire story.

Dawn had broken. And so did her heart.

CHAPTER FOUR

*Seldons have only one care: their
own unruly passions.*

A TRUTH UNIVERSALLY
KNOWN BY ALL DALES

Owle Park, 1810

"Rather ironic it was Preston who kept you from being ruined," Crispin pointed out.

Hen looked up from where she was examining the bottles on the shelves and tried to ignore his slight, but she decided to turn it to her advantage. "You might have learned a lesson from him."

"From Preston?" Crispin snorted.

"Yes, well, if you had followed his example, you would have been able to stop your cousin from seducing my brother." She smirked a bit, especially at his outrage over having the entire Henry and Daphne debacle laid at his feet.

Never mind that her brother was deliriously happy with his Dale bride.

"How was I to know what lengths your brother would resort to if only to ruin her?"

"He *married* her," Hen pointed out. Something Crispin had failed to offer when he'd asked her to run off with him.

"Marriage is no guarantee of happiness," he muttered.

Hen couldn't argue with that. In fact, she silently agreed with him. How her life might have been different if only . . .

"I tried to meet you," Hen told him. "I would have gone to Paris with you."

"Actually, I've always been a bit relieved you didn't," Crispin offered. "Whatever would I have done if you had been caught up as I was? No, it was better that you remained in London."

For Crispin hadn't come home as he'd planned.

And all the while she'd waited, her fury at Christopher knowing no bounds.

But even that had faded once any hope of Crispin's ever returning was lost.

Bletcher House
Surrey, 1805

"Lady Astbury?"

Henrietta turned around slowly. She'd come down to dinner early, for there wasn't much to primping and dressing when one could only wear black. "Yes, Lord Michaels?" She smiled slightly at the rake. Not to encourage him but to tease the fellow a bit.

She shouldn't even have been attending a house party, but when the invitation had arrived, she'd hardly been able to refuse—not when she'd learned that her hosts had engaged a noted tenor to sing for the party.

Besides, it was only another month before she'd be out of her weeds for good, so it was hardly that unseemly for her to appear in public.

Not that her mourning period had mattered much to the rogue's gallery of suitors who had been sniffing about since Astbury's accident—including this handsome devil, Lord Michaels, the baron being one of her more persistent admirers.

"Lady Astbury," the baron repeated in that sultry voice of his, a rich, deep baritone that left her shivering.

Of all the men in her circle of admirers, she found him the most intriguing.

In another time, Lord Michaels would have been the sort to catch the eye of a Virgin Queen, his sharp tongue and sweet words convincing her to finance his pirate adventures. In fact, it was rumored that was exactly how one of his forebearers had managed his barony and the family fortune. This Michaels had inherited not only the title and the money but also the infamous Michaels features—bright eyes, a hawkish nose and dark, coal black hair.

The man had left a wake of swooning ladies and broken hearts in London, but Hen alone had remained aloof to his overtures.

Her grief—she told herself—so raw and fresh was what was keeping her heart from being engaged. But that was merely the lie she told herself to keep from admitting the truth.

She was still waiting for another. As foolish as that might be.

Rather like her flirtation with Michaels. Though she did like the way he made her laugh. Forget her misery, which for the last few months had wound around her like an unbreakable chain—having lost her mother, her husband and then her father in quick succession.

And yet here was Lord Michaels, writing her poetry. Foolish bits of nonsense, so that she couldn't help but be touched.

Perhaps this poetic streak was what had finally convinced old Queen Bess to raise up the first upstart Michaels.

"Have you heard?" the baron teased. "That there has been a horrible mistake with supper."

That caught her attention. "A mistake?"

"Yes," he told her, coming into the empty drawing room. "A most dreadful one. Our hostess—" he shuddered a bit, and Hen knew exactly what he meant.

Lady Bletcher was a horror—a dim-witted flibbertigibbet who could barely order a proper tea, let alone arrange a complete supper. But what did one expect when Lord Bletcher had been married three times, with each wife considerably younger than the last?

And if it was possible, sillier than her predecessor.

The newest Lady Bletcher was no more than seventeen, an ornament merely, and worse, a *cit's* daughter who had brought an enormous dowry to her marriage and now fancied herself quite the tonnish Original. And her knowledge—or, rather, lack thereof—of the simplest matters such as precedence at the table was shocking.

And honestly, no one of any consequence would have accepted the invitation to Bletcher House, the earl's country seat, if it hadn't been for the fact that Lady Bletcher's money had enabled the infamous newlyweds to bring Menghini to entertain at their house party.

So treasured was Menghini's voice that he refused to sing to the usual large audiences of the grand playhouses and insisted on performing only for small, select parties.

And even then, only those who could afford his exorbitant demands.

Hen would have gone and stayed with that aged harridan Damaris Dale to have had this opportunity to hear the infamous Italian sing.

"It isn't Signor Menghini—"

"No, no, the fellow is all well and good. Proud sort, rather fussy. When I went by the dining room he was explaining to Lady Bletcher that he must have the most bland of meals to keep his throat in balance." Michaels snorted, as if that was the most amusing notion he'd ever heard.

Hen would have pointed out that Signor Menghini's very purse depended on that throat, so perhaps the man's demands were rather important to him.

"So if it isn't Signor Menghini, then what has dinner in such a state of disarray?" she asked.

"Someone has finally explained precedence to Lady Bletcher." He shook his head woefully.

"About time," Hen said without thinking.

Michaels laughed. "Yes, that may be so, but it also means you and I are now separated and you have a new dining companion—other than Lord Bletcher." He waggled his brows at this, for it had been the baron who'd guessed rather astutely as to why Hen had been invited—Lord Bletcher thought she might make an excellent fourth Lady Bletcher in the event this one turned up her toes as quickly as the other Lady Bletchers had done.

While the baron continued to smirk, Hen ran through the list of guests and tried to determine who might be beside her.

"I'll give you a hint," Michaels offered. "Some viscount has usurped my spot—demmed cheeky fellow. Just arrived. Distant cousin of some sort of Lord Bletcher's, but I think it's the flimsiest of connections, and one made only to hear that Italian sing."

Hen smiled. She had been about to do the same thing— stretch the branches of her family tree before her invitation had arrived.

"He's a pompous fellow," Michaels was saying over his shoulder from where he'd stopped to examine the small collection of books on one wall. "But everyone is making such a fuss over him all because he managed to escape the demmed Frenchies."

Henrietta's world stopped. "*Escaped?*" Her insides quaked at the very word, and she drew her shawl tightly around her shoulders.

No, it couldn't be. Still, why couldn't she breathe? Why was the floor suddenly spinning?

"Yes," Michaels said, pulling a book off the shelf, completely unaware of her turmoil. "Got caught in Paris when the Peace failed in '03. Been locked away ever since. Foolish of him being over there to begin with. Never saw any reason to cross the Channel. Nothing but foreigners over there."

Henrietta shook her head. Not so much at Michaels's own pomposity but at the growing blaze of hope that had ignited in her heart.

Escaped.

What if it was him?

She glanced away and indulged in a familiar remembrance—his lips upon hers. The very scent of him. This wasn't the first time she'd drifted back to that night, yet now she wondered if her memories, after all this time, were more fanciful than truly real.

Could a kiss have been so . . . so . . . unforgettable?

Hen drew in a deep breath. And here she'd vowed, promised herself, to forget him. She'd had to. When it had appeared that all hope had been lost, she'd had no choice but to bow to her family's expectations and marry Astbury.

Astbury . . . Henrietta flinched a little at his memory. While she'd been overly fond of the marquess, it hadn't been a marriage based on love for either of them.

And his kisses?

Oh, they'd been satisfactory, she supposed—but there never had been that breathless sort of destiny when Astbury had kissed her, the sense of being claimed like when Crispin Dale had teased his lips over hers . . . when his hands had roamed deliberately, possessively, over her body.

Just then, the rest of the guests arrived, as well as their hostess, who had come to announce dinner. Hen found herself quickly scanning the faces.

Hoping.

"Should I be jealous?" Michaels asked, having returned to her side.

"Pardon?"

"You appear to be looking for someone."

The fellow was far too astute—and practiced, she supposed. "Of course. You know how I love a good diversion."

He waggled his brows at her. "Later on, I could be most diverting."

Henrietta made the sort of snort that her Great-Aunt Zillah was infamous for—a huff of amusement and derision all at once. "I'm hardly looking to be diverted," she told him, even as she watched the rest of the guests arrive.

All to no avail.

But she was rather used to the hopelessness of it all, and she forced a smile upon her lips as she had so many times since Crispin Dale had left London with her heart.

CHAPTER FIVE

How do you know a Dale is lying?
When they give you their word.

THE SELDONS' FAVORITE SAYING

"Ah, there you are, my lord! I thought we'd lost you," Lady Bletcher was saying as two late arrivals appeared in the dining room. She bustled the man to his place at the table and said, "May I present your charming dinner partner, Lady Astbury."

As the mysterious fellow turned around, Henrietta's heart stopped.

Crispin.

The same and yet so utterly changed.

"My lord," she managed, dipping into a short curtsy.

"Lady Astbury," he said, bowing slightly so his gaze never left hers.

There was a sniff from behind him, and the viscount stepped aside to reveal his great-aunt, Damaris Dale.

She sniffed again, spared a scant, yet scathing, glance at

Henrietta, then followed Lady Bletcher down the table to her place near the vicar and Lord Juniper's spinster sister.

Henrietta barely gave the lady any regard, for she was too busy taking in every detail of Crispin: his hair, falling long about his shoulders and barely trimmed; how his jacket was too big on his spare frame; then, finally, the set of his jaw.

Determined and unyielding.

And it seemed he was doing much the same as he studied her, for she saw very clearly the exact moment when he took in her mourning gown and his brows tilted. "And my condolences on the loss of your—"

"My father," she replied.

"Yes, yes," their feather-headed hostess chimed in, having returned from her duties. "Poor Lady Astbury, just out of mourning for her departed husband when her father leaves her back in weeds yet again. How lucky for you that black becomes you, Lady Astbury." The lady smiled as if that boon made up for all of Henrietta's grief. "Oh, dear, there is the Italian. Bletcher wants him made to feel most welcome. With what we are paying him I should think it would be the other way around." She heaved a sigh and departed.

Up and down the grand table, people were finding their seats and greeting each other, but to Hen there was only one other person in the room.

Him.

"You got away," she said, feeling the hot sting of tears in her eyes. She dashed at them before they made their unruly appearance.

"I promised I would come back," he replied, holding her chair for her. "Yet you married him. Astbury."

Henrietta sat down quickly, for in truth, it felt as if her legs were about to give out. "I tried to come meet you . . . that morning. Christopher caught me and—"

He took his own chair and shook his head slightly before quietly saying, "It was better that you didn't."

For if she had succeeded, whatever would have happened to her when the Peace was broken?

And there was one other matter. That nagging question that she'd never been able to resolve, no matter how many times she recalled his kiss. Recounted his words.

Had he intended to carry her off to Paris to marry her or just ruin her?

Not that any of it mattered now. He'd come home. Safe and whole.

"I thought you were lost forever," she said quietly.

He shook his head. "Just misplaced for a time," he replied as if he'd just got back from his hunting box in Scotland.

Misplaced, indeed! Henrietta couldn't help herself, she smiled. How could she not when his blue eyes sparkled with mirth and his lips—oh, those wondrous chiseled lips—turned just so.

He was as roguish as ever—much to her delight.

Slanting a glance at him, desire—not the innocent sort she'd known when last they'd met but passion, raw and full of need— shot through her limbs.

As if he knew she was watching him, he turned and met her gaze with a sultry look that burned through her.

They stared at each other, lost in the wonderment of rediscovery, until the lady on the other side of Crispin, the Marchioness of Knapton, caught hold of his hand and nearly

tugged him into her lap. "Dear, dear Lord Dale, I am posi-
tively dying to hear an account of your escape from France. Is
it true you took the jailer's wife as your mistress in order to
effect your release?" The lady's wicked tones implied that she
would like to be the next seduction on his list.

"Lady Knapton, you know a gentleman never tells such
secrets. Nor would I ever besmirch a lady's reputation."

"Of course he wouldn't," his Aunt Damaris declared from
the far end of the table.

"Ah, but her husband's honor?" a heavily jowled fellow—
Lord Morton, Hen thought—from across the table chuckled.
This was followed by male laughter all around.

Henrietta turned a wry eye to Crispin. "How did you
manage to escape, Lord Dale?" she asked, doing her best to
appear coolly indifferent to his story.

"As has been stated—with the help of a lady," he replied.
"But not as some of you would think. It was Lady Sinclair
who was my savior."

"Lady Sinclair? Why, she's nigh on seventy some years,"
Lord Morton declared.

"Eighty," Crispin corrected. "I shared my cell with her
husband. As you know, Bonaparte only ordered the arrest of
Englishmen—not our ladies."

"Only decent thing that Corsican has ever done," one of
the other lords at the table blustered.

"Hear, hear," agreed the rest of the gentlemen.

Crispin nodded. "After Lord Sinclair was arrested, his
wife came to Paris all on her own."

"Dear heavens!" the marchioness exclaimed. "Whyever
would a lady do such a thing?"

"Love, Lady Knapton," Crispin told her. "The dear baroness loved her husband more than anything, and she couldn't stand the thought of him in a French prison . . . Or worse, dying there alone."

"Always was a demmed headstrong gel, that Maggie Campbell. Sinclair was a lucky bastard to have won her hand," one of the older gentlemen added.

Crispin smiled. "She bullied and cajoled and bribed the guards daily to see that our bare necessities were met. Even then, they would only let her come to the bars of our cell for a few minutes each day."

Henrietta looked away, as did some of the other ladies, if only to dab at their eyes in admiration of this brave lady and her unfailing love for her husband.

"Then Lord Sinclair took a turn for the worse. He had a heart ailment before we were arrested—a dank cell and wretched food didn't help matters."

"Poor dear," the vicar's wife murmured, though no one was really listening—not with every head turned toward Crispin.

"Finally it became clear he hadn't much time left, and Lady Sinclair became even more determined." He glanced down at the wineglass before him, as if the rich red wine was a hypnotic elixir.

"Whatever did she do?" Hen said softly, prompting Crispin out of his trance.

"Yes, well, one day Lady Sinclair arrived at the cell and the guard opened the cell door for her—something he had never done before—allowing her the freedom to be at her husband's side. Poor Sinclair was failing fast and hadn't even been able to rise the day before to greet her as he usually did."

Crispin paused for a moment, as if the memories were too much, and it was all Henrietta could do not to cover his hand with hers and offer him whatever comfort he might find.

But how could she with his aunt right there—watching her as if she'd been a serpent at the table?

"This is so terrible," Lady Knapton declared, sniffing indelicately into her napkin.

"Yes, it did seem the end was very near," Crispin agreed. "After she kissed her husband's forehead, she turned and handed me her cloak." He paused again. "I took it, as any gentleman would, but then she said the impossible. 'Put it on, my lord,' she bid me. 'Put it on and leave in my stead.'"

A stunned silence filled the room, as if they couldn't quite believe it.

Crispin heaved a sigh. "Then Sinclair, weak as he was, added his own insistence. 'Leave me alone with my wife to say a proper good-bye, you pup. Can't do anything licentious with you lolling about.'"

There were a few laughs at this, especially at Crispin's attempt to match Sinclair's rich brogue.

"What did you do?" one of the ladies asked.

"As a gentleman, I would think you refused her," Lord Morton insisted.

"Yes, of course I refused her," Crispin replied. "Then she drew me aside and put my hand to her breast. 'I haven't much time either,' she told me. And indeed, there was a large mass there. A cancer." He shook his head. "'There is no hope for me,' she continued, 'but at least let me spend my last, *our last* hours, as fleeting as they may be, together.'" He glanced up and looked around the table, his gaze pausing only for a second on Hen. "There was no guarantee either of us would see the end of the day if Lady Sinclair's deception was discovered. I would still have to, by the grace of God, make it out of the prison without someone noticing that I wasn't the baroness—but to give her more time, I gave her my jacket, and she added her hat to my costume—some grand plumed thing," he said as he waved his hands over his head. "Good God, however do you ladies manage to balance such monstrosities atop your heads?"

His theatrics managed to break some of the somber, heavy air that had descended around the table.

"So you escaped," Henrietta prompted.

"Of course he did," his Aunt Damaris interjected. "He's here, isn't he?"

"Only because of Lady Sinclair's ingenuity," Crispin corrected. "For you see, the baroness was as thorough as she was brave. She'd sewn a purse filled with gold inside her cloak. Good gold coins—the likes of which the French haven't seen since they chopped off their king's head. And somehow she'd managed papers for me—excellent forgeries that claimed I was a merchant from Calais, giving me the perfect excuse to make for the coast."

"You do have the look of a peddler about you, Dale," one of the fellows joked, and everyone laughed.

After a bit, Henrietta asked the question on everyone's mind. "What became of Lord Sinclair and his brave wife?"

"I didn't leave Paris until I knew her ladyship was safe—one way or another." He glanced down at the table for a moment of silence, for there wasn't anyone who didn't know what that meant. Then he looked up and glanced over at Hen.

"They were granted the only thing they ever wanted, Lady Astbury, which was simply to be together. Against all odds. Until their final day together."

And Henrietta had the sense that Crispin Dale was no longer talking about Lord and Lady Sinclair.

"To Lady Sinclair," Lord Michaels said, raising his glass in a toast, and everyone at the table silently followed suit.

Signor Menghini's talents were as everyone claimed—extraordinary—but Crispin heard barely a note of the man's elegant, rich tenor.

He had eyes only for the woman seated a few feet ahead of him.

Lady Astbury.

So she'd married him. Regret filled his heart. He should never have left London without her.

Of course, in hindsight, he should never have left to begin with.

What was it Sinclair had so often said? *A man's true fate is to acknowledge the choices he makes.*

And, he supposed, the choices his Calypso made as well.

Crispin sighed and restlessly sat back, earning him a scathing glance from his Aunt Damaris.

That did nothing to diminish the myriad of questions running through his head, all of which would remain unanswered as long as the Italian continued to sing of lost love and tender reunions. The irony was not lost on Crispin, nor was there anything he could do but wait patiently for the demmed fellow to stop his endless warbling.

And he was quite positive it wouldn't be quite so interminable if only Henrietta would turn around and look at him. Dinner had been torture enough—sitting so close beside her, so close he could inhale her perfume, count the slight hint of freckles on her nose, feel the brush of her sleeve as she turned to speak to him. Torment all.

But what he desired most was her glance. One look.

The sort of look he'd only ever shared with her. A glance that told him exactly what was in her heart.

Hadn't Sinclair told him, *You'll never go wrong if you follow your heart, my boy.*

Demmit. For to follow his heart was in many ways more perilous than a French prison.

Especially with Aunt Damaris at his side. But to his delight, his great-aunt was so overcome by the singing—a miracle in itself, given how particular she could be—that she was too busy sharing her admiration with the equally enthralled matron beside her to notice him rising from his seat at the conclusion and deliberately strolling past his Calypso, his siren.

Crispin held his breath as he glanced over his shoulder at her.

And then their eyes met.

Swift and hot, passionately. There was an intimacy that had never been there before.

Or perhaps he'd forgotten. Smiling at her, and seeing the light in her eyes spark, he knew he would not have forgotten this . . . this deep sense of belonging.

But he also realized immediately that they were no longer the starry-eyed youths who had found each other by accident.

Nor did she need any prodding to follow him this time.

He continued toward the door, and he heard her making her excuses to the lady beside her—claims of a megrim and the need for her dear Poppy to mix up a tea that would do the trick.

Crispin continued down the hall until he came to a small parlor, where he slipped inside and waited.

A few moments later, he heard her footsteps lightly pattering after him.

But then, to his dismay, she didn't appear at the door.

"Oh, bother," he heard her mutter out in the hallway.

And when he looked out, he spied her tugging at the hem of her long gown where it was caught on the base of one of Bletcher's many standing suits of armor.

So much for being subtle and discreet.

She glanced over her shoulder at him. "Well, don't just stand there. Help me."

Crispin laughed and hurried to her side, unhooking her skirt. "Why is it I always have to rescue you?"

Henrietta, after glancing down at the state of her gown, smiled at him. "I do believe it is your destiny."

He shook his head. "No, this is." Catching her hand, he tugged her inside the room, closing the door after her.

And in an instant, she was in his arms and he had her pressed against the door, their lips tangled together, hungrily—as if this quickly sparked passion between them was the first bit of air they'd been able to find in years.

Nor had the years diminished the desire that blazed between them against every bit of good sense they both possessed.

He was the Dale of Langdale, and the lady in his arms was a Seldon—no matter what name she bore.

Yet how she ignited his soul, claimed his heart with her touch, her hands splayed out across his chest, catching hold of the lapels of his jacket and tugging him closer, her hips brushing close, inviting him, calling to him, welcoming him.

After years of dreaming of this moment, so many dark, cold nights spent holding onto the hope that one day, somehow, he'd find a way back to her, here she was, as willing as he'd imagined—more so.

For now she was a woman grown.

True to her passionate Seldon nature, she'd already unbuttoned his jacket, was tugging open his waistcoat, and her hands—warm and soft—found their way to touch him, explore him, seeking him.

And all this time, they kissed. Lips forged together, tongues dancing over each other, moving over each other, prodding and teasing in anticipation of what was to come.

What they both desired.

Crispin gave in to his every fantasy, desires that had haunted him all these years, and he tugged at her skirt, pulling it up so he could catch hold of her, pull her close, press himself against her cleft.

She moaned and shifted again, a brush like a cat seeking her pleasures, begging to be stroked, petted, caressed.

He indulged her, indulged himself, stroking her soft, supple thighs, exploring the soft curls at her apex, and when she shifted again, opening up to him, he pressed forward until he found her very core—hot, wet and quaking with need as he touched her, explored her, running a finger over the nub there and teasing her to open up.

And this woman, no longer a figment of his imagination, whispered the words he'd longed to hear.

"Make me yours, Crispin. Please."

Hen was afire with need. But then again, she'd spent the entire evening lost in what had seemed an impossible dream.

Crispin making love to her. Inside her, filling her, claiming her until she was just like this—panting for want of what she knew not.

From the moment he'd tugged her into his arms, she'd melted, surrendered any bit of good sense she possessed to discover if her years of secret, torrid dreams were true.

Hen quickly discovered dreams were ethereal and hardly made of the muscled, solid strength that surrounded her, possessed her, commanded her—especially when he touched her, teased her so.

And yes, she couldn't help herself, she pleaded with him. *Make me yours.* She realized she no longer cared about ruin, or scandal, or marriage. Listening to his story, she would have sworn he'd risked everything for this moment, this dangerous chance.

How could she deny him now, when it was a desire they shared?

Ever so much.

Even now, she had the sense he was seeking something deeper than just passion. Something they'd lost that early dawn when she'd tried so desperately to be with him—and failed.

"Please, Crispin," she whispered, running her hands across the front of his breeches, letting her fingers slide along the length of him.

He was hard and long beneath her touch, and she shivered with anticipation, catching his bottom lip with her teeth and nipping at him as she opened the buttons that held him back from her.

One by one, until he was freed and his solid length thrust into her eager grasp.

She glanced around them, trying to see where this could be done, how they could manage this, *now*, this very moment.

Crispin, she discovered, was as impatient as she, and he hitched her leg around his hip, pinned her to the door and found his way to her opening, thrusting inside her, leaving her gasping for air.

He filled her, quickly, hard and fast, and Henrietta would have let out a loud, eager moan if he hadn't covered her mouth with his.

Thus they were joined—precariously, Crispin thrusting into her, sliding over her sex, leaving her gasping, while his tongue teased and taunted her.

Henrietta had never imagined this . . . this wild, hungry dance. The solid door behind her, the hard, ravenous man covering her, filling her, claiming her.

Again and again, he thrust into her, and Henrietta grew more and more breathless. Her need rising, her desires leaving her coiling tighter and tighter, closer to him, closer to the reward that beckoned her.

"You are mine, Henrietta Seldon," he told her, promised her, binding her with his words and then with his body, as he thrust hard and sure into her and sent her willingly into the bliss that had been awaiting them for far too long.

A taste of heaven that she'd never known.

Crispin carried Henrietta to the low wide settee in the corner, cradling her in his arms and settling them both in the velvet cushions.

Mine.

He'd meant it.

Henrietta's eyes were half closed and she had a lazy, happy smile on her lips. "I didn't realize it could be like *that*."

"You didn't know?" he asked, realizing what she was saying.

She nuzzled closer to him. "You did that to me. Thank you ever so much." She made a sound like a cat purring for more.

Crispin grinned and was ready to oblige her, feeling ridiculously proud that he'd been the one to take her over the edge, put that contented look of bliss on her face.

Her hand cupped his chin. "If you hadn't gone to France, we might have been doing this for years now," she chided with a grin.

"Yes, yes. I know. My Aunt Damaris reminds me of my folly any occasion she can work it into the conversation. Which is nearly constantly."

Henrietta didn't blame the old girl. "When I heard that Bonaparte had ordered arrests—" She looked away.

"You thought me lost," he realized.

She nodded. "After the peace accord ended, I waited a year, thinking you couldn't have been caught. Arrested. I did everything I could to put off my parents, delay a betrothal that had been in the works since the day I was born. Gave every missish, petulant excuse I could devise to keep from marrying Astbury because I had no word of what had happened to you." Henrietta sighed and looked away.

"What changed?" he asked.

"I couldn't live with the not knowing. I'd become utterly desperate . . . that is until I saw your cousin, Philomena, at a soirée."

"Oh, you wicked girl," he laughed, knowing exactly what Henrietta had done. "Poor Cousin Phi."

"Yes, well, it is common knowledge that she's rather near-sighted—"

"So you resorted to subterfuge." He shook his head.

"The Foreign Office would have been quite impressed," she told him, smiling smugly. "I came over to where she was standing—"

"With all the other wallflowers—" he guessed.

She shrugged. "Yes."

"And *you* posed as one of them?"

The idea of Henrietta Seldon blending into the spinsters and forgotten souls of the walls was hilarious. It was like a lioness standing amidst a field of mice.

Henrietta sniffed at his doubts. "As I said, the Foreign Office would have found it a most convincing effort."

"Not so when the object of your deception can't see past her nose."

Henrietta scrambled to sit up from where she'd been nested in his arms. "I needed news of you. Would you rather I knocked on your Aunt Damaris's door and demanded an accounting of your whereabouts?"

Crispin sputtered. "You would have stopped her heart."

Now it was Henrietta's turn to laugh. "I'll make sure to never mention that to my Aunt Zillah—she'd come calling before the day was out."

"They do despise each other, don't they?"

"That's an understatement," Henrietta agreed as she curled back into his embrace.

They both laughed a bit, for the two old girls hated each other with a vehemence that bordered on the unholy, and they would do everything in their power to keep Henrietta and Crispin apart if they ever suspected there was even a hint of affection between the pair.

He shook his head and didn't want to consider Aunt Damaris's opinions. Not now. "Yes, well, so you came up to my poor blind cousin and did what?"

"I acted as if we were old friends and asked how her cousin fared in France." Henrietta turned away, for the words still rang in her ears.

I fear we have little hope of ever seeing him again.

Henrietta drew an unsteady breath. "That's what she said," she told him, her voice wistful. "I thought you lost."

"Never. Not when I had you in my heart. You were my star. My siren calling me home each night," he told her, kissing her lightly on the forehead, his lips eagerly moving down to capture hers again.

They kissed, their bodies stirring anew, until outside in

the hallway, the sound of voices stopped them both cold.

"I will find where my nephew has gone, and I will find him now!" This was followed with a grand *huff*. "It is imperative I stop him before he goes mad."

"Oh, good God! Aunt Damaris!" Crispin said like an oath, righting them both as he got to his feet and immediately set to work straightening his clothes.

Henrietta followed suit. "What if she—"

Crispin put a finger to his lips to silence her, for neither of them truly wanted to face *that* scene. Henrietta quickly set to work hiding the evidence of her dishabille.

"He went down that hall not long ago, madam," one of the footmen intoned.

"Find him!" the lady ordered. "He's in terrible danger."

From behind him, Henrietta whispered in his ear, "Am I dangerous?"

"Utterly," he replied, turning around and taking her into his arms for one last moment. "You've stolen my heart."

As Aunt Damaris's determined footsteps rang louder, Crispin looked around the small room for some place to hide Hen, but there was nowhere, save the dark gardens beyond.

Apologetically, he nodded toward the set of French doors. "Do you mind?"

She laughed quietly. "What? And escape your aunt's wrath? I'd walk through hell merrily rather than face that old—" She snapped her lips shut, then clapped her hand over her mouth as if she needed added insurance not to finish that sentence.

Not that Crispin didn't know exactly what she had been about to say. "Yes, I know. *Old dragon*. We call her that as well—but only behind her back and only if one is well north of the Scottish borders." He kissed Henrietta once more, then prodded her out the doors. "I'll come to your rooms later."

Henrietta's eyes sparked, and she blew him a kiss before quickly melding into the night.

B y the time the door to the salon swung open, Crispin had already settled himself in a chair by the fireplace.

"Whatever are you doing?" Aunt Damaris demanded.

"Aunt, I never thought of you as one to pry into a gentleman's business."

"Where is she?" Damaris came barging into the room, searching about, even in the corners.

"Who?" Crispin asked.

"You know who," she shot back as she looked suspiciously at the garden doors.

"Hardly. Especially if I have to ask. Twice."

"Don't be coy with me, boy. I've known you since you squalled your first. I saw how you looked at her. A Seldon, Crispin! A Seldon."

"A Seldon? Truly? And me without a pistol at the ready." He rose from where he'd been sitting and nodded for her to take the grand chair.

There was nothing Aunt Damaris loved more than a good throne from which to scold.

"Don't jest with me," she said, moving to the chair, since her search had been fruitless. "This is most serious, Crispin. What that upstart little *cit* was thinking seating you next to the likes of her—"

"You mean Lady Knapton?"

"No! Lady Astbury—who, but a few Seasons back, was Lady Henrietta Seldon."

"No," he gasped in mock horror. "Then it is a good thing I found her incredibly dull-witted. But then again, all the Seldons are an ill-bred lot, aren't they?"

"It didn't look like you were bored to me."

"I was merely being polite." He settled into the other chair and stuck his long legs out in front of him, as if settling in for a good coze.

Aunt Damaris snorted. "You were intoxicated by that Jezebel."

"I hardly think Lady Astbury qualifies as a—"

"A Jezebel, I say. And you were flirting with her. She unfortunately possesses all the beguiling airs her Aunt Zillah used to prance about town—and look at her. Lady Zillah Seldon has never married, but oh, the houses she's gained over the years, and not in the proper way." The lady's brows rose. "Her niece is no different."

Yes, he got her point. But that was Lady Zillah, not Henrietta.

Yet his aunt wasn't done. "Oh, Crispin, what did those wretched Frogs do to you that would make you forget the basic tenants of being a Dale. And you, *the* Dale."

"I assure you, Aunt Damaris, that any hint of interest I might have showed Lady Astbury was naught but a momentary lapse in judgment. A trifle, a meaningless dalliance over dinner—"

"Just make sure it stays that way. Another few courses and she would have had you spellbound with her Seldon wiles.

Don't tell me you've forgotten what happened to Ruston Dale? He was never quite right after he was seduced by that witch Yolande Seldon. He had to be restrained."

"I do believe that had more to do with the fact that he was prone to fits."

"*Harrumph!*" Aunt Damaris deplored being contradicted. Or thwarted. Still, she adjusted her course ever-so-slightly. "You have your lineage to consider. Your duty."

Translated, his aunt's words were clear: As the Dale of Langdale, he was obligated to ensure the family line.

And not with a Seldon.

Yet when he looked at Henrietta Seldon, he saw everything he wanted in his viscountess. A lady of beauty and wit. Noble and intelligent.

She'd grace his life, his house, his heart, with a fiery passion, one he'd spent the last few years of imprisonment and deprivation promising himself he'd gain once he was freed.

If anything, that hope, that tiny spark, had carried him through the years of captivity.

But given the look of abject horror on his aunt's face, he knew he needed to placate her. "Lady Astbury is a widow. Certainly not the sort I'd consider for marriage." He glanced down at his nails as if bored beyond distraction by this entire conversation.

"I would hope not," Aunt Damaris said, then she smiled at him, a faint, weary tip of her lips. "I worried so for you, my boy. What would come of all of us if we'd lost you? And if you were to—"

She stopped short of saying the words.

If you were to marry one of them—

"You shall not lose me, dear one," he said, taking her hand and laying a gentle, gallant kiss on her fingers. "Now off to bed with you. Why Cousin Prudence hasn't seen you to bed hours ago, I don't know."

"I'm not a child to be coddled or bullied," she shot back.

"Be that as it may, if Prudence won't take care of you, I'll replace her with Philomena–"

"Enough!" Damaris protested, for they both knew that as nearsighted as Phi was, she wasn't as malleable as Prudence Dale, Phi having inherited an excessively stubborn streak from her non-Dale mother. "I'll go, but only on the condition that you swear, Crispin—"

"Swear what, Auntie?"

She wagged a finger under his nose. "That you stay away from that dreadful woman."

Crispin laughed. "Do you doubt that I would? Aunt Damaris, I would think that at your age, you would know that a gentleman will flirt, he might even have improper dalliances, but when it comes to marriage, family is first."

"You have a duty and obligation to marry," she reminded him yet again as she went to the door.

"Auntie, this I swear: While I will only marry for love, my duty to you and the family will always remain of the utmost importance."

Improper dalliance . . .

Henrietta had heard enough and turned from the garden windows, moving quickly along the side of the house.

Grief, and its all-too-familiar blackness, closed in around her.

She'd known better than to listen at the door, for her mother had always said nothing good ever came from eavesdropping, but she had to know what Crispin was going to say to his aunt.

She had to know what was in his heart.

Especially after she'd spent all these years wondering if he had wanted her for marriage or . . .

And it was all as she feared. She was naught but a dalliance after supper to him.

How like a Dale to use their pretty words and lying hearts to get what they wanted.

And here she'd worried over him, cried for him, carried her secret love for him all these years. Felt a traitor for marrying Astbury only because her heart had belonged to another.

That horrible year his aunt had spoken of—it had nearly killed Henrietta. And now she discovered he thought of her merely as a dalliance?

Wretched, lying Dales. Curse them all, she fumed.

But foremost in her thoughts was how to get as far away from Crispin Dale as she could. She never wanted to see the man again.

And woe to him if he ever did cross her path.

Ill-bred lot indeed! She'd show him exactly how ill-bred she could be.

And in this state of fury and a blinding need to lash out, she raged around a corner and nearly bowled over a tall figure out for an evening stroll.

"Well, well, what have we here?"

Henrietta glanced up to find Lord Michaels stubbing out a cheroot, grinning at her unlikely arrival. "I had thought you weren't—"

It really didn't matter what he was going to say, for Henrietta needed to know something very important. "Lord Michaels, am I a dalliance to you?"

"A wha-a-t?" he managed, taking a step closer to her, taking in her tumbled appearance, his eyes narrowing.

"You heard me, a dalliance?"

His features shifted from the rakish demeanor of a few moments earlier to an expression Hen hadn't thought him capable of.

"No," he said, simply and plainly. "Never, my dear Lady Astbury. I'd carry you to Gretna Green this very night if I thought—"

And in a very impetuous, Seldon sort of moment, she made the most scandalous decision of her young life.

"Then take me."

CHAPTER SIX

If the wind has changed, so has a Seldon's heart.

WELL-KNOWN DALE MAXIM

Owle Park, 1810

Crispin got up from where he'd been sitting on the steps and paced the short distance across the cellar. "Michaels?! Of all the madcap, idiotic—"

Henrietta held up her hand to stave off the rest of Crispin's censure. Hadn't she heard much the same from everyone of consequence in her life since the day she'd made her fateful decision to run off with the fellow?

And they were all correct. It had been a disastrous decision. For her. And for Michaels—whose heart, very much like her own, had belonged to someone else.

What a pair they'd made.

"I will never understand why you married that bounder," Crispin said, taking a bottle off the shelf and examining it.

Hen sighed. It was all so complicated. More so now than it had been then. "You know why."

Crispin stalked back toward her, bottle in hand. "That doesn't mean I understand. If only you'd trusted—"

"Trust? A Dale?" she shot back. "It has been drummed into me since birth that trusting a Dale is like trusting the devil."

"As faithless as a *Seldon*," he shot back.

Hen flinched a bit. "I was willing to look past your name."

"Look past my name?" He set the wine aside and crossed his arms over his chest, stubbornly defiant. "It would have been *your* name."

She rose to her feet to face him, unwilling to let him tower over her. "And that of our child's," she snapped back before she could stop herself, her darkest secret spilling out. She clapped her hand over her mouth, as if that could put the words back where they belonged—locked tightly in her heart.

Yet there they were. Spat right out in the open.

In the cool shadows of the cellar, her secret brought a light that left them both frozen and blinking at its stark glare.

Crispin's eyes narrowed. "Our what?" he asked in a cold, quiet voice.

"You heard me," she said, wishing yet again she could learn to curb her impetuous tongue. Then she repeated it, this time a little more gently, for the memory was, even after all this time, still raw. "Your child."

Crispin shook his head. "How could that be—we only—"

"Yes, once. But that was all it took." She turned away from him, wishing she'd never blundered into *this* mire.

"But you were married," he argued, "to that bounder. How could you even think—"

She whirled back around. "Think that my baby was yours?

I knew it for certain." She laughed a bit. "Michaels was no bounder. Contrary to what everyone thought of him, he was actually quite harmless."

"Harmless?" Crispin's expression was incredulous. "The rumors I've heard of his exploits—ruinous deeds that aren't fit for a lady's ears, not even those of his widow." He said all this while wagging his finger at her.

Henrietta blew out a long sigh. "If you are referring to the gel in that Southwark stew, she was paid to tell that story. As were countless others." She reached over and gathered up the wayward pup, settling the little mutt into her arms. When it looked up at her with sleepy eyes and nestled closer, content with being safe and sound, Henrietta smiled.

Exactly like Michaels. A wild, reckless reputation, when in truth the man had been like this pup—content to sleep beside her, but nothing more. She'd been his perfect foil. A widow from a family infamous for its passionate nature, with a lady such as Henrietta beside him, who would ever suspect . . .

"He never . . . We never . . ." She hated to say any of this, for one hint otherwise would ruin the baron's perfectly crafted reputation. And yet . . .

Didn't this man before her deserve some portion of the truth?

She closed her eyes, yet that only brought a myriad of memories—stark images from a long ago night. Hours of labor. The midwife's grave expression. Michaels's pale glances. And the silence . . . that horrible silence when there should have been lusty cries announcing a new life.

Crispin's eyes widened with shock. "You expect me to believe he never—"

Her hand fluttered in a distracted wave at him. "Yes, that is exactly what I'm saying. I knew the child I carried was yours because I never was a true wife to Michaels. He never wanted me like that. Me or any other woman."

Crispin gaped at her, that is until his expression changed, slowly, a dual understanding dawning in his eyes.

But one only really mattered.

"A child," he said as if testing the words.

"Yes. *Our* child." Henrietta hugged the puppy to her chest and bit back the tears that came as she remembered the little, still form that had been quietly wrapped in a swaddling blanket by a grief-stricken Michaels and taken from her.

Suddenly even the warmth from the puppy in her arms was too much, and she gently set it back in the basket, dashing at the tears forming far too quickly for her to quell with her last remaining bit of resolve.

But this time she wasn't alone.

"Ours, Calypso?"

She nodded, biting back tears. "A daughter."

He crossed the space separating them and quickly wrapped her in his steady, sturdy embrace.

"My dearest Calypso, why didn't you tell me?" he whispered into her ear as his hands stroked her hair, smoothed away the shivers of cold, icy memories of that horrible, wrenching night.

She clung to him, as she might have then. Sought the solace that was so overdue. "I tried. Don't you remember?"

CHAPTER SEVEN

*When a Dale comes to call, count
the silver and your daughters.*

A SELDON WARNING

London, 1808

"Tonight, Crispin," Aunt Damaris reminded him for about the hundredth time as he helped her down from her carriage. "Lady Portia Claybourne is perfect—even if she isn't a Dale." She glanced around at the other arriving guests and nodded at an acquaintance. "Despite that misfortune," she continued, "the Claybournes are well respected, and as the daughter of the Earl of Lindsey, she will grace Langdale with a regal air that has long been missing."

Crispin ignored that jibe. For his own mother hadn't been a Dale—or the daughter of an earl. Or even a viscount. The lowly offspring of a poor baronet, she'd won his father's heart, and together they'd enjoyed a bright and happy union.

One Crispin had been holding out to find since he'd reached his majority.

"Lady Portia Claybourne," Aunt Damaris sighed yet again as they climbed the stairs into the ballroom. The way his aunt said the chit's name made it sound as if the earl's eldest daughter was the salvation of their family.

Which she wasn't, Crispin would point out. The Dales needed neither her dowry nor her lofty connections.

"Yes, indeed, Crispin, it is time to put all your reckless ways aside. Forget Paris and see to your obligations."

While his aunt was correct that it was time for him to find a bride, it hadn't been his imprisonment in Paris that had left him "reckless," as Aunt Damaris liked to refer to his roguish reputation about town, but the returning to England, the being tricked and deceived by his Calypso, trapped by her siren ways and left adrift when she fled to another's embrace that had been his undoing.

He'd left Bletcher House done with dreams and hopes and wishes and had turned instead to amorous pursuits, gambling and fast horses, hoping to leave behind what had happened.

Forget *her.*

He'd spent three reckless years trying to shut her out of his life, gaining a reputation as one of the *ton*'s most unrepentant rogues. Yet eventually even the most beautiful and willing ladies of London lost their luster, their tempting shine, and Crispin faced the simple truth: It was time to forget and marry another.

Still, Crispin found himself loathing the prospect ahead, especially since her family was expecting it. His aunt certainly was. And so, most likely, was Lady Portia.

All that was left was to form the words and see the deed done.

A proposal of marriage.

How hard could it be to get married? Henrietta Seldon had done it twice now—with nary a glance behind her.

Crispin cringed. He had to stop thinking about *her.*

His Calypso. His siren. The golden-haired beauty who haunted his dreams.

But when he entered the Knolleses' ballroom, his practiced gaze sweeping the room, to his shock and dismay, he found himself staring right at the very lady he vowed to forget every single day.

Then again it was demmed hard not to see her, for she stood all alone, as if Society had drawn a wide circle around her and decreed that no one cross that boundary—for every lady in the room was obviously giving her the cut direct.

And yet proudly, and all alone, she faced them down with her usual grace and nobility—as if she hadn't noticed in the least that she was being shunned.

"Upon my soul!" Aunt Damaris gasped when she too spied Henrietta. "Not her!"

That was all his aunt had to say. *Her.*

For when Aunt Damaris said it, it came out as if she was choking on the devil.

For in his Aunt Damaris's estimation, Lady Henrietta Seldon was probably as close to hell as one could gain in this world.

Certainly Henrietta was creating havoc in his heart, tangling him up and leaving him doubting his own resolve.

I don't care about you anymore, he would tell her.

But it was a lie, nonetheless. And she'd know it.

Always would be, he realized as he watched with a twinge of jealousy as Lord Juniper strolled right up to Henrietta and greeted her as an old friend. That was until the man's mother came furiously barreling through the crowded room and tugged her besotted son away.

"The fool!" Aunt Damaris spat out. "Why he continues to loiter after her when he knows—why, everyone knows—just what a ruinous jade she is!" Then she turned to Crispin, her eyes narrowed and searching. "Come now, Crispin," she said, nudging him out of his spellbound state—literally with the sharp end of her fan. "There is Lady Portia. How lovely she looks. Like a fair, blessed angel." She towed him in that direction. "Don't you agree?"

She asked this as they came to stand before his chosen paragon and he found himself forcing a smile to his lips.

It hadn't been this hard before.

Before. . .

Crispin couldn't help himself; he glanced over his shoulder in her direction.

His long-lost Calypso.

Demmit, whyever had she run off with Michaels? He was of half a mind to stalk over there and demand an explanation. He deserved that much at the very least, didn't he?

"So you've noticed who is here," Lady Portia's mother said with a decided sniff of disapproval. "Whatever is she thinking, coming out in Society? And with her husband barely cold."

"Cold?" Crispin asked. "Michaels is dead?"

Beside him he could feel his aunt flinch, and he glanced over at her—just quick enough to see her try her best to hide her guilt.

She'd known. Of course she had. This was Aunt Damaris.

"Yes, cold. Poor, dear Lord Michaels," Lady Lindsey was saying. "Fell from his horse and died—not three months ago. They say she drove him to it." This was followed by a significant glance over at the newly widowed Lady Michaels. "How can she appear in public like that? And in a red gown, no less! Does she think that is proper mourning? Someone should tell Lady Michaels . . . no, I can't even use the word *lady* in the same sentence as that creature."

"No one can with the likes of them," Aunt Damaris agreed.

Crispin glanced again at the object of so much scorn and thought she looked pale and drawn. Hardly the carefree Jezebel she was being made out to be.

"It is scandalous," Lady Portia agreed. "Mourning should never be mocked thusly. It shows a want of proper breeding." The girl shook her head. "I don't know why she would even consider coming out when it is obvious no one will dance with her."

At those three words, Crispin stilled.

Dance with her.

They sang with an impossible tug at his heart. Pried a wedge inside it. Reopened a bottle of desire he'd furiously pounded a cork into.

Had drank and gambled and whored himself nearly to death in hopes of forgetting.

He looked over at Henrietta Seldon and knew forgetting

would never be possible. Not when she stood there, defiant in her red gown, her chin tucked up at a noble angle, as if she had merely deigned to make an appearance, not risking everything by coming here.

Dance with her. It was a clarion call that he couldn't shake free. Couldn't ignore. His boot edged forward and then came to a practical halt.

No, he didn't dare do this.

"It is only a matter of time before she takes a hint and leaves," Lady Portia added with another sniff—very much like her mother's haughty disdain.

This time when Crispin looked over at the very perfect and proper face of the lady who, up until a few moments ago, he'd been nearly certain was to be his viscountess, he saw her in a new light.

And it was hardly flattering. Instead of seeing his world graced with well-heeled manners and an aristocratic sense of place and honor, he saw instead a lifetime curbed by restraints.

Then he looked at Henrietta and felt his heart soar free.

"Yes, whoever would be so foolhardy to go near her now? She's put two husbands in early graves. Gracious heavens, what would she do to a third?" Lady Lindsey asked, to which there were nods all around.

Save Crispin, because he could imagine quite perfectly what she would do for him. Knew all too well. Open his world up beyond the strictures that his aunt and just about everyone around him wanted to impose upon him now that he'd, as his aunt liked to say, "finally come to his senses."

What was the point of being the Dale of Langdale if he couldn't rule his own destiny?

Much as Henrietta Seldon had always done with hers.

It was something that he admired about her, as much as it drove him to distraction.

Then she glanced up and looked him directly in the eye. The challenge in her glittering gaze, the pride that held her fast and dared him to come claim her—it was more than he could resist.

Calypso, his Calypso. His again. His always.

That hope, that dream pitched him forward—deaf to the protests rising in his wake.

Besides, she owed him an explanation. Or two.

And then they could make up for lost time before she got it in her impetuous head to run off with another rogue.

Save one.

Him.

Henrietta watched Crispin start across the crowded ballroom. It had only been by chance that she'd discovered that he was going to be here tonight. A stray comment over tea at Aunt Zillah's afternoon in.

Lady Portia Claybourne is to be commended. Her first Season and she's making a most advantageous match. A most proper one.

Henrietta assumed this bit of news was more a slight on her own social history than it was the bit of gossip it might outwardly appear to be. After all, it had taken her three Seasons to "catch" Astbury, and then there was her most improper elopement with Michaels.

Still, the gossip appeared to be one of the newer bits being bandied about by the *ton*, for there were approving smiles all around Aunt Zillah's drawing room at the news until one of the ladies made the benighted mistake of mentioning the groom-to-be in a Seldon home.

"A most handsome fellow—Lord Dale," Lady Weybridge declared. "I do believe his aunt had despaired that he would never start his nursery—what with that horrible business in France and all his devilish ways . . ."

There were nods all around, some disapproving and others with a slight smile over the viscount's exploits.

"I, for one," Lady Weybridge continued, "will be at Lady Knolles's soirée tonight, dreary as such company is, if only to witness the happy announcement. Who doesn't love seeing a rogue of the first order finally being tamed."

All the others twittered with excitement, though not Aunt Zillah, who glowered at having a Dale being bandied about her parlor. Meanwhile, Henrietta tried to breathe.

Crispin? About to be engaged?

No, it couldn't be.

But to her dismay, the chatter—as it was wont to do—shifted again, and Henrietta was left floundering and grasping at nothing more than those spare tidbits.

Worse yet, she could hardly ask Lady Weybridge for more details. Not in front of Aunt Zillah.

Instead, she had to sit with her hands folded in her lap and do her best to appear quite bored by it all.

That is, until she came up with a likely excuse to escape and scurry back to the Seldon town house on Harley Street, where she frantically sorted through the huge stacks of invitations on the long-neglected salver; Christopher barely deigned to show his face in proper Society—and Society was probably more than relieved for that small measure of good fortune—and Henry could have cared less about soirées and balls.

Especially when hosted by such low *ton* as Lady Knolles.

But to Hen's great delight and even greater horror, there it was, printed on thick vellum: an invitation to Lady Knolles's soirée.

Henrietta stared down at it for what seemed like an eternity before she straightened, steeled her spine and marched upstairs, ordering Poppy to find a dress that might fit her thin frame—then adding, "Nothing in black," much to her long-suffering maid's horror.

She'd never quite recovered from the loss of her child, then Michaels's shocking death had left her ever so thin and drawn. But Poppy, true to her loyal nature, clucked and flitted about, doing her best to ensure her mistress appeared to advantage.

Yet deciding a thing and doing it was turning out to be an entirely different matter. While Hen had known her arrival would be met with some degree of disdain by the more stuffy members of the *ton*, she hadn't expected to be given the cut direct by everyone in attendance.

Well, not everyone, she reminded herself. Lord Juniper had come over to give her his regards. Dear, kindly Gusty—always her greatest champion—had come directly to her side, that is until his mother had dragged him away.

And now here was Crispin prowling toward her.

When he'd first arrived, she'd done her best not to rush to his side, relegating herself to simple glances in his direction, until she hadn't been able to stand it any longer and had blatantly stared at him.

Look at me. Oh, please, Crispin, forgive me.

And then he turned, his eyes meeting hers, and all her regrets about coming tonight drifted away.

Still, it was nigh on impossible to believe he was truly coming toward her. He couldn't be . . . It would be too scandalous. But given the look of pure horror on his Aunt Damaris's face, Hen realized that was exactly his intent.

Despite those horrible words he'd said that night.

. . . a momentary lapse in judgment. . .

. . . Ill-bred lot. . .

. . . a meaningless dalliance. . .

Oh, bother, why had she come here? He was most likely coming over to toss her out as a favor to Lady Knolles. She was naught but a momentary lapse to him and always would be.

But what if that isn't the case?

Her insides fluttered as that spark of hope kindled inside her. What if she'd been mistaken that night? Overheard him wrongly? She tried to catch her breath, which suddenly seemed caught in her throat. This was the moment she'd been waiting for. And yet . . . whatever would she say?

I was a fool. I was ever so mistaken.

Besides, wasn't this what Michaels had urged her to do as he'd lain on his deathbed?

She drew a deep breath and exhaled, letting her heart ring with the words that she wanted to say aloud but had never dared. *Crispin, you are my heart and soul. Could you ever. . .*

. . . love me?

Henrietta uncurled her hands, which had knotted into

two tight fists. She must be prepared to discover that it was too late for them. She'd seen to that.

That didn't stop Michaels's reassurances from coming hauntingly to the forefront of her tangled, panicked thoughts.

"Dearest girl, go to him. Forget all this Dale and Seldon nonsense. Live the life I never could have had—free to love as I might. The one you've spent far too long running from."

And so she'd come to London. Far too early to be proper. Something she knew Michaels would have approved of heartily.

Then again, he'd never been one for proper. Apparently neither was she. For here she was, a Seldon in love with a Dale.

Then the terrible moment of truth arrived as Crispin stopped in front of her and they stared at each other.

She should say something, but words failed her. The last time she'd seen him, she'd been in his arms, shivering with passion.

Yet now . . . oh, bother, she was trembling like a leaf for altogether different reasons.

He inclined his head slightly. "My lady."

She dipped into a curtsy. "My lord," she managed.

"Dance with me." He held out his hand.

He couldn't have said anything that could have shocked her more. It was one thing to come over and acknowledge her but quite another to ask her to dance.

Together.

In front of everyone.

"Calypso, take my hand."

Calypso? That name said more to her than anything else. If she was still his siren . . . his Calypso . . . might he?

She wouldn't know until . . . Reaching out, she let him capture her fingers. Immediately, that familiar spark of recognition ran its wild course up her arm. If he noticed, he only paused for a second before folding her hand into the crook of his arm and guiding her out to the dance floor.

Henrietta didn't look left or right. She ignored the whispers, the wild flutter of fans, the blatant stares, as well as the plain old ill-mannered pointing.

He'd come to claim her, and all she could do was follow her heart.

CHAPTER EIGHT

Marry a Seldon and regret the rest of your days.

A DALE CAUTION

"You've been unwell," Crispin said, more than shocked at how thin she'd become, how frail she felt in his arms.

"There have been some difficulties," she murmured, glancing away. "But they have passed. It is just that—"

"You don't have to speak of it if you do not want to," he rushed to assure her.

She nodded and offered no further explanations.

But before she turned her head, he saw that tiny spark in her eyes extinguish in an instant at the very mention of her situation.

What the devil had that bastard Michaels done to her? Crispin would murder him on the spot if the cheeky fellow hadn't already stuck his fork in the wall.

And where the hell were her brother and that good-for-nothing nephew, the Duke of Preston? Why hadn't they seen to her well-being?

He ground his teeth together. It was all unpardonable.

Yet he couldn't leave well enough alone. "Calypso—" he began even as she whispered his name, "Crispin—"

Their names entwined together, lifting up through the ballroom as if the Fates had always bound them just so.

And when Henrietta looked up at him, he knew. For there it was once again, starting to flicker to life. That light that was his and his alone.

He couldn't help himself; he grinned wickedly at her.

Still, he had to ask. Had to know. "Why, Calypso?"

"Why what?" she asked, glancing away again.

He tugged her closer. "You know what."

She shivered a little, and how he wished she wouldn't tremble so.

"That night," she began slowly, "at Bletcher House. I heard you. You and your aunt. I overheard what you said about me."

Crispin could feel his brows pull together as he thought back to that night. Both unforgettable and horrible. And he remembered. "Oh, good God! You believed that?"

"Well, yes," she told him, her gaze lifting to his again as if she was searching for something. "You said—"

"I know what I said. How could you believe me so faithless? Especially right after—"

She glanced away. "I wanted to believe it wasn't true, but you and I, us, our families, there is so little trust—"

He knew exactly what she meant. How he'd hated her the

next morning when he'd learned that she'd run off with Lord Michaels.

As faithless as a Seldon is what the Dales said.

Looking at the evening from her side of the door—where, he would point out, she was eavesdropping—he supposed the Seldons had much the same opinion of his relations.

More to the point, however could she have known what was truly in his heart when he'd never said the words?

Never had the chance, if he was being honest.

Still . . . "Whatever did you expect me to say to my aunt?" he asked. "She was already in a pet over the seating arrangements. Should I have just added to it by telling her that I was madly in love with Lady Henrietta Seldon and that I planned to marry her?"

She stiffened in his arms. "If that was what you truly meant to do—"

He leaned over and nuzzled her neck, caring not a whit that every gossipy cat in the *ton* was watching them. And for her ear and hers only he whispered, "Do you have to ask, Calypso?"

This time when she looked up, he knew there would never be doubt in her eyes again.

"But why didn't you just—"

He laughed and shook his head, swirling her around in a tight circle as they navigated the other couples. "And how would you have told your family?" he posed. "Marched into supper and declared your intentions to marry me over the second course?"

"Not," she told him, her eyes alight with mirth, "if I didn't

want to see the third course served up in the nearest asylum."
She bit her lips together to keep from laughing, but her eyes,
it was always her eyes that were the path to her soul, and
how—right this moment—they sparkled!

The merry sight illuminated his heart with hope.

Whatever sadness was encamped within her would heal.
With laughter and love. Of this he was sure. He would see
to it.

"If you must know, I was going to break our news to Aunt
Damaris slowly," Crispin offered.

"From a hunting box in Scotland?" she teased back.

"I had thought Ireland," he replied and then laughed.

"Too bad you didn't consider such a strategy tonight,"
Henrietta pointed out, nodding in Damaris's direction.
"Hardly subtle, my lord."

He dared a glance over at his great-aunt and got no further
than the horrified tilt of her brows. And more to the point,
she stood alone, Lady Portia and her mother having left. "Yes,
well, I suppose I've made a muddle of things, haven't I?"

At first Henrietta didn't answer, and then ever so quietly
she said, "Not to me."

"I had to save you, Calypso," he confessed, then smiled
again at her. "How is it you are always in some fix or another?"

"I have no idea," she teased back. "Nor do I have any
notion as to how you are going to repair this muddle."

"I do," he said with every ounce of certainty he possessed.
"Tomorrow we shall marry."

If he hadn't been holding her so tightly, she would have
stumbled over her feet.

"You can't—"

Crispin smiled for all to see, as if she'd just turned the most elegant set he'd ever had the pleasure to partner. "You heard me. Marry me. Tomorrow. Be at the archbishop's office at half past three and the good man will marry us himself. Then and there."

He felt the shivers run down her frame, rattling her down to her boots, and he felt this niggling sense of foreboding—a dark shudder which he immediately set aside and ignored.

Especially when she warned, "This will cause a terrible scandal."

"I expect nothing less," he agreed, more than ready to take on the family maelstrom this would surely ignite.

And with that, the musicians ended their playing and the dance concluded. There was nothing left for Crispin to do but bow over her hand, for he could see quite clearly Aunt Damaris thundering in his direction, a concerned-looking Lord Juniper hot on her heels. "Until tomorrow," Crispin told Henrietta hastily.

Henrietta must have seen the approaching horde as well. "Until tomorrow," she promised before she quickly disappeared into the crush of guests behind them.

"Ah, dear Crispin," Aunt Damaris declared when he arrived at her house the next morning.

Her welcoming and dulcet tones did not fool him.

Not in the least. "I have come as you summoned, Aunt Damaris." He folded his arms across his chest and waited in the middle of her morning room.

"It was hardly a summons," she said, waving her handkerchief at him and nodding toward the chair closest to hers. Then she flicked a glance at Prudence and sent her poor, beleaguered companion from the room.

Crispin deliberately took a spot on the settee across from her. "What can I do for you?"

If there was a flicker of annoyance in her eyes, she hid it quickly enough. "What do you intend toward that gel, Crispin?" his aunt asked, getting directly to the point.

And they both knew she didn't mean Lady Portia.

"I am going to marry her."

He couldn't have said anything that could have shocked his aunt more.

With too much grace to let her mouth fall open, her expression gradually and slowly turned to stone. Hard, unyielding granite.

"I forbid it," she told him. More than once she'd made such a decree to various Dales—the cousins and distant relations over whom she kept an ever-vigilant watch. And every single Dale had done as she'd ordered.

And while he might be the Dale of Langdale, this was Aunt Damaris, and no one naysaid her.

Until now. Realizing the futility of any argument he might make, Crispin rose. "Then I suppose our interview is over."

Aunt Damaris rose as well, quickly enough that it belied her advanced years. "Crispin, please. Consider what happened to Duncan Dale—he married that Seldon witch and the authorities burned him for her deviltry. And what happened to her? She married the magistrate."

"That was three hundred years ago, Aunt Damaris. Besides, Lady Michaels has never shown the least inclination toward the black arts."

Save beguiling his heart and soul.

"Lady Michaels! Bah! You can call that Seldon whatever you like, but she is still one of *them*. However can she be a proper bride for you in comparison to Lady Portia? She's been married and widowed twice now. You would wish *that* on us?"

"That" meaning his assured demise. That his title would go to the next in line. Dilbert Dale.

That did stop him for a moment—the vision of Dilbert, his silly wife and their seven rambunctious children trampling through the graceful halls of Langdale was more than horrifying. But his pause lasted only for a moment.

For he saw an entirely different future. One filled with passion. With children with Henrietta's bright eyes. Of a house once again filled with laughter.

With love.

For how long had it been since the hallowed halls of Langdale had rung with merriment? Too long.

"She holds my heart," he told his aunt. "She has for years. And I won't let her go this time."

There it was. The truth of the matter and, as far as he was concerned, the end of this discussion.

His honest, earnest words startled his aunt, and absently she sat back down, her hand catching hold of the armrest as she settled into her familiar throne.

"And that is your decision?" Aunt Damaris asked quietly, her gaze fixed on the fireplace mantel, where a row of miniatures of the most prominent Dales was displayed.

"Yes, Aunt Damaris."

"When is this to be done?"

"Today," he told her.

"Today?" she gasped.

He nodded, then patted his jacket. "I am meeting Lady Michaels at the archbishop's office at half past three. Already got the Special License, and His Grace will marry us on the spot."

"So quickly?" she managed, more to herself than to him.

"Yes," he told her firmly. "I don't expect your blessing—"

"And you won't have it," she shot back. Then she heaved a sigh. "But I won't lose you either."

She reached over and picked up the bell, ringing it for Croston. When her butler appeared at the door, she told him, "Take Lord Dale to the cellar and allow him to choose whichever bottle of my father's wines he prefers." Then she glanced up at Crispin. "My wedding gift. But don't consider it a sign that I agree to any part of this madness, and don't you ever dare bring that woman to call on me."

Crispin nodded. "Thank you, Aunt Damaris."

She waved him off and bid Croston to send in Prudence.

Crispin followed the butler to the cellar door, a hallowed portal among the Dales for it led down to where Aunt Damaris stored her father's extensive and legendary collection of wines.

It was an unexpected gesture of concession from his aunt, and though he hardly had time to creep about the cellar and find the bottle he'd longed to open for years, Crispin wasn't about to turn down his aunt's offer and risk raising her ire further.

Croston opened the door for him and was about to lead the way down the steps when Prudence came rushing along. "Oh, my! Croston, herself is demanding you return upstairs immediately."

The butler glanced over his shoulder at her and then at Crispin, his expression never changing. Such was the life of anyone employed by Damaris Dale—being ordered in one direction and then yanked in another.

"I can find my way, Croston," Crispin assured him, taking the candle from the man and making his way down the steps.

"You can now," Prudence said as she closed the door behind him and locked it.

"Miss Dale!" Croston gasped.

"Orders, Croston. He is to be left in there until he comes to his senses."

Croston regarded the door warily, but he didn't make a move toward it, despite the pounding from his lordship within.

It was Damaris Dale who paid his salary, and if the old girl thought her nephew was in peril, then this was for the best.

Hen paced outside the archbishop's office while Poppy stood patiently at hand.

"You aren't doing yourself any favors, my lady, by waiting," her maid told her. *Again.* "If you are seen—"

"Yes, yes, I know," Henrietta told her. And Poppy was

right. It was rather unseemly for her to be loitering about in front of the deanery when she truly had no reason to be there.

At least none that she could share.

"Mayhap he isn't coming," Poppy offered, looking over her shoulder rather than saying the words to Hen's face. Saying exactly what they were both thinking.

For here it was nearly four and there was no sign of Crispin. He'd been here earlier. That much she knew. For the fellow at the desk had grudgingly admitted that his lordship had come first thing in the morning, obtained a Special License and spoken directly to the archbishop.

So there it was. Exactly as he'd promised. He would arrive. No matter what.

Hen looked up and down the street once again despite her flagging confidence.

"It is starting to rain," Poppy pointed out, tugging her own pelisse tighter around her neck. "Your hat will be ruined."

By reflex, Hen's hand went to the fetching new bonnet she'd just gotten this week. It was ever so lovely and would, as Poppy said, be ruined with the least bit of rain, but for once Henrietta Seldon couldn't care less.

"'Tis barely a sprinkle," she replied, knowing she would stay put in a downpour if she must. Still, she wrapped her own cloak closer, pressed her lips together and blinked at the sheen of tears forming in her eyes, the ache inside her chest like the loss of Crispin's child all over again. Her heart breaking in two.

Not to mention the ruin of a brand-new hat.

Worse, it wasn't like she could run to Henry or Christopher and cry foul. That Crispin Dale had left her at the altar.

She knew exactly what they'd say—after they got over their dumbfounded shock—*good riddance.*

And what would Aunt Zillah tell her? *You expected one of them to keep their word? Bah! I thought you had more sense, gel.*

And just when she was about to skulk off and lick her wounded pride—or at the very least save a most expensive hat—a carriage came rollicking around the corner at a break-neck speed.

Her heart skipped, and she threw a triumphant glance in Poppy's direction.

Being the practical sort, Poppy made a loud sniff that said in so many words, *We'll see.*

The carriage came to a quick halt in front of Hen, and immediately the door swung open.

But it wasn't Crispin stepping out.

"Gusty," she exclaimed as Lord Juniper stepped down. "Where is—" she stopped as she looked over his shoulder and realized there was no one else in the carriage.

"So sorry, Hen. Came as soon as I could muster," he told her, doffing his hat and bowing. Then, as if remembering the task at hand, he patted his coat until he found what he was looking for and pulled out a folded note.

She took it reluctantly, for a note, dear heavens—that couldn't bode well.

But she held out hope, for Crispin had promised. Vowed. Sworn nothing would keep them apart.

"So sorry, Hen," Gusty told her, stepping nearer Poppy so Hen would have some privacy.

Dear Lady Michaels,

    I have been remiss in offering you my protection when it wasn't mine to give. I am already promised to another, and by the time you have read this, she shall be, as intended, my wife. I therefore give you leave to find another and wish you well in your endeavors.

    Crispin, Lord Dale

Hen read the note twice, then crumpled it up and threw it into the gutter. "This is a lie." Then she turned to Gusty. "Take me to him."

Her old friend shook his head. "Can't, Hen. Got that from him myself. 'Tis too late."

She shook her head, and this time the motion rattled free the tears that had been threatening to fall for the last desperate half hour.

And there was Gusty. Warm and familiar. Folding her into his arms and patting her gently as if he feared she would shatter into a thousand pieces.

Which she thought she might.

"I'll never marry again," she told him between sobs.

"Now that would be a demmed waste, if you don't mind me saying," Gusty told her.

"I'm a horrid wife. I send men to their graves."

And to other women, but that part she wouldn't say aloud.

She glanced away, loathe to admit even this. "I am ruined, Gusty. They all cut me last night. Even the lowest of the *cits*." She sniffed. "All save you and . . ." Well, she couldn't say *his* name. "They scorned *me*. I know 'tis all my own fault, but I never thought—" She swiped at her nose, conscious of Gusty's well-fashioned jacket. "Oh, dear. Whatever must you think of me? I might as well move to the country and die alone surrounded by cats just like my ancient Aunt Netty did." She glanced up at him to see what he thought and found him smiling at her.

"Now, now, a bit of time in the country might be the right idea. Especially with a respectable husband at your side."

"Bah!" Henrietta stepped away from him, suddenly aware that she was—once again—making a public spectacle of herself. "No one will have me. That was evident last night. Not even Lady Knolles will deign to invite me again."

"And why would you want to go to such a dull affair?" he asked, straightening. "As for no one wanting you, that's balderdash. I've always wanted you. Still do. Would marry you right this moment if you'd only say yes. Then we'd shake off these London cats and leave them to their gossip. You can live the life of a queen well away from their tattling. I'll see to it. I promise."

Brokenhearted and lost, Henrietta looked up at the man who had been as much a part of her life as Henry and Christopher had. A good friend. A kindly soul. A more respectable gentleman couldn't be found.

And when Gusty promised a thing, Hen knew he'd keep his word. Unlike other purported gentlemen.

Then she saw all too clearly her way out of all this.

Marry Gusty. Be Lady Juniper. Live in the soft green hills of Kent at Juniper House well away from any Dales.

After all, what had she always wanted? A good life in the country. Images of Owle Park flitted through her thoughts—a graceful house surrounded by green lush meadows and the lulling song of birds. Juniper House, if she remembered correctly, wasn't much different.

Better still, a life with Gusty would be well away from the folly that was passion . . . and love.

Lord Juniper must have seen the fleeting bit of hope in her eyes, for he caught hold of her hand and turned her so she faced him.

"Marry me, Hen," he implored, gathering her up in his arms, sheltering her from the rain and from her worst fears—that she no longer had a place in Society. Or more to the point, in Crispin's heart. "Marry me now," he rushed. "If anything so we can get out of this dreadful drizzle." He laughed a little. "I've always been prone to the sniffles, so if you don't say yes quickly, I'll hold you responsible for the dreadful case that is sure to come from a damp cloak and wet boots."

CHAPTER NINE

Love is a many splendored thing.

MR. MUGGINS, IF HE COULD TALK

Owle Park, 1810

"You can't be serious," Henrietta said, taking a sip from the bottle of wine Crispin had plucked from the shelf and opened. "Your Aunt Damaris locked you in her wine cellar for three days?"

Crispin shuddered. "Yes, until Cousin Matheus came to call. Poor fellow, when Croston left him unattended in the foyer, he thought he was going mad when he heard my pounding from the cellar. Managed to get me out—though in return Aunt Damaris scratched his name from the family Bible."

Henrietta laughed and held out the wine for him.

He took a long drink. "It wasn't funny. By the time I got out, you were good and married, and well away from London."

"How was I to know that note wasn't in your handwriting?" Henrietta asked.

"Or that my aunt had sent Juniper in my stead, knowing full well his feelings for you."

She glanced over at him. "Why didn't you marry Lady Portia?"

Now it was his turn to laugh. "She wouldn't have me. Or so Aunt Damaris swears. I never did see her again." He sighed. "And with you married to Lord Juniper, I hoped, well, I supposed you might finally be happy."

Hen shook her head. "How could I be so, when I wasn't with you?"

They sat there for a time, each silently regarding the other, until Crispin spoke again. "What did happen to Juniper?"

She closed her eyes. "Contrary to what his mother likes to claim, I neither bewitched him nor poisoned him."

"And don't forget my personal favorite, drove him mad," Crispin added, tipping the bottle in a mock salute.

"It isn't funny," she told him starchily, snatching the bottle from his grasp and taking another sip. "When Gusty said he was susceptible to taking the sniffles, it was no jest." She set the bottle down and rose from where she stood, pacing about a bit, the memories nipping at her heels. "By the time we'd married and were in the carriage to Juniper House, he was already claiming the damp would be his undoing." She paused. "And it was. A fortnight later, he was gone."

"From the sniffles?"

"No. Pneumonia," she shot back. For it was hardly a matter to be teased about. "He went so quickly. And then there was his mother making all these horrible accusations. I might have believed them if it hadn't been for his brother, Eustace."

"The one who inherited?"

"Yes. Dear boy that he is, he confided that Gusty had nearly died twice before of the very same thing and he'd been complaining for nearly a month before we married that he wasn't feeling well."

"So when he died, how come you didn't return to London?"

"How could I? I feared seeing you with her. And then there was Aunt Zillah. She bundled me up after the funeral and hauled me north to her house outside of Buxton, and before I knew it, nearly a year had passed. She told me I couldn't go back to Harley Street until I could prove to her that I would be a proper widow."

Crispin laughed. "Have you ever been?" He took a drink and waggled his brows at her.

"No," she said, retrieving the wine and taking another drink. It was truly an excellent vintage.

"Yet you returned to London," he said, coming to sit beside her.

She nodded. "I had to. Preston was making a shambles of everything. Henry arrived last fall and insisted I come home. Dragged me, really. Claimed I was the only one who could nag some sense into Christopher."

"Seems to have worked."

Henrietta laughed. "Miss Timmons was none of my doing. Preston managed her all on his own. And rather well done, if I must say. She is the perfect duchess for him. For all of us."

Crispin glanced over at the puppy still asleep in the box. "Save her choice of hounds."

Henrietta laughed, and eventually so did Crispin.

"And so the wrongdoing between our families returns in some grand circle, doesn't it?" she pointed out, nodding toward the little mongrel.

"I suppose so," Crispin said, his words wistful. "But I propose that this time, it ends differently."

She glanced up at him. "How so?" she asked, feeling a bit shy suddenly, and a bit dizzy from the wine.

It was the wine, wasn't it?

"Instead of launching our two families into a new feud for the next three hundred or so years, what if Mr. Muggins's roguish behavior is the beginning of a new accord?"

"What sort of accord do you propose?" she asked, slowly and carefully.

"Marriage." That single word came out in a defiant thrust.

Immediately, Henrietta was shaking her head. "I cannot. I'm horrible at marriage."

Wasn't three husbands good evidence of that?

"I disagree," he replied.

He would.

"Those marriages were made for all the wrong reasons," he pointed out. "And you were only truly married to one of them."

She couldn't argue that—Juniper had fallen ill before they'd reached the inn for their wedding night.

Still . . . "Crispin, I don't see how we dare."

"We must," he insisted, getting to his feet, catching her hand and pulling her against him. "I don't think I can live with being responsible for another of your madcap marriages."

She shook her head at his teasing. "But . . . but . . ."

"No, no buts," he told her. "For once, let your heart be your guide." And then he kissed her.

When his lips touched hers, she realized she'd been waiting all this time for him to do just this. Kiss her.

It had been so long.

His lips claimed hers, and there was nothing she could do but open up to him. His tongue teased over hers and she sighed, her arms winding around his neck, pulling him closer.

She couldn't . . . she shouldn't.

And yet how could she resist, especially when he deepened his kiss, his fingers pulling her hairpins loose and letting the long strands fall down over her shoulders. As the strands fell free, all her fears tumbled away as well.

And when he loosened her gown and slid it down her shoulders, kissing and nuzzling his way down her neck until suddenly his mouth closed over one of her nipples, the ripples of desire racing through her limbs chased at the remainder of her doubts.

"We don't dare," she tried to insist, struggling to find some solid ground beneath her wavering legs.

Crispin's response was a loud snort of derision and then a kiss, this time lower, over her belly and then lower still.

"Oh, don't you dare," she said as he grinned up at her from where he now knelt, her gown puddled around her feet. "Crispin, this is ever so wrong."

But this was Crispin Dale, rogue that he was.

And so he did.

Dare, that is.

"Well, yes," Henrietta managed as his breath blew hot

over her already wet sex. "Yes, well, that is anything but wrong."

The doorbell to Owle Park rang loud and clear through the house.

It took Mrs. Briar a few minutes to toddle up to it and answer it, and when she did she was more than a bit shocked to find a lofty-looking gentleman standing there, hat in his hand.

"I am Halwell. Lord Halwell. Here to collect Lady Juniper."

Mrs. Briar gaped at the man. "But you've already been here." Then she looked out in the drive, where yet another carriage sat—this one an impressive traveling barouche that was rich and well appointed.

While the other one . . . well, it had only been a curricle. Hardly the sort of carriage for a trip to London.

Suddenly doubts began to assail the poor lady.

"Been here? Hardly," Lord Halwell blustered. "I've been delayed. A vexing bit of trouble with one of the braces. Now if you will summon Lady Juniper for me—" He nodded toward the stairs.

Mrs. Briar glanced at the stairs as well and then shook her head slightly. "But I thought—"

"Is Lady Juniper here?" he pressed as if he was starting to doubt he'd come to the correct address.

"Well," Mrs. Briar told him in her usual forthright way, "I don't rightly know where she is."

"**D**id you hear that?" Crispin said, glancing up from his delightful task of leaving Henrietta Seldon shivering with pleasure.

"It sounded like the bell," she said with a flutter of her hand and a distracted glance at the stone steps up toward the door.

He nuzzled the spot between her legs again, where she was still quivering from the first time he'd "wronged" her. "I do believe your rescue has arrived."

She glanced down at him. "I don't want to be rescued. Not now."

He pulled her into his arms and laid her down upon the floor. The stones were dry and cool against her heated body.

"What do you want?" he asked her.

Her hands slid up and ran through his hair, cupped his hard, square jaw. "You, my love. Only you." And to show him how much she wanted him, nay, *needed him*, she nestled beneath him, one of her legs winding around his hip, her hands opening his breeches, stroking him once she'd freed him, guiding him to her.

Crispin smiled and entered her slowly, tantalizingly, leaving her restless beneath him. Even as he filled her, he moved again, pulling himself nearly out of her, his long, hard length sliding against her. It was pleasure and desire and agony all at once.

She'd come so quickly, so hard and fast when he'd teased her with his lips, his tongue, his mouth, but now that he was inside her, it was as if he wanted to discover every bit of her. Tease her. Explore her.

His hand curved around her bottom and drew her closer, thrusting deeply and completely into her, leaving her gasping, "Yes, Crispin. Oh, yes." Her eyes fluttered open and her gaze met his, and in that instant she realized everything that had been missing all these years. Everything she'd ever longed to know.

It was all there, shining in his eyes. His love for her. His desire to see her sigh and cry out beneath him. His need for her—a mirror of her own for him—a sense of completeness that had been missing from her life.

In that quiet, gentle moment she understood what she had longed for.

What she'd been running away from for far too long.

And Henrietta Seldon, siren of his heart, let go of all her fears and finally discovered the beauty that was making love.

An opening and sharing of one's heart and soul.

And when she found her release, it was with Crispin's gasp and deep thrust inside her carrying her upward and over, tumbling together into a bliss of their own making.

Some time later, Crispin leaned over and kissed Henrietta on the nose. "Calypso, I have loved you since the first moment I saw you."

Henrietta sighed, then suddenly her brow furrowed. "The first moment you saw me?"

"Yes," he replied, putting another kiss on her forehead.

She sat up, a mulish expression coming over her once dreamy features. "The first moment you spied me, I was down over a log with my backside up in the air and you were ogling me."

"Yes, be that as it may, I must confess I found you quite bewitching at that moment. Such a lovely bum. How could a man not fall in love with such beauty before him?"

She swatted at him. "You are horrible, Crispin Dale—"

He hardly seemed to notice her ire. "Yes, well, come kiss me again. I'm in the mood to be most horrible yet again." His brows waggled at her.

"Oh! You Dales!" Playfully, she pushed him away.

"Seldons!" he shot back as he caught her and once again covered her body with his.

"Crispin?" she asked as he started to nibble at the most distracting spot behind her earlobe.

"Hmmm?"

"When we get married—we are getting married, aren't we?"

"Yes, with banns and the vicar and all proper."

Henrietta smiled at this. It sounded rather lovely. But still she had to ask. "When we get married—"

Crispin stopped his nuzzling and met her gaze. "Yes?"

"Might we hyphenate our names? You know, Lord and Lady Seldon-Dale?"

His horrified expression answered her question.

"Yes, well, I suppose not. Let's just start with the wedding," Hen offered.

"I believe this qualifies as the wedding night," he told her, and then he showed her how eminently qualified he was to make good that promise.

For a Dale.

Harriet Hathaway has only one wish when it comes to love: to marry the Earl of Roxley. But wishing for his heart and keeping it, Harriet will soon learn, takes more than casting up a whispered desire to earn a perfect happily ever after.

Continue reading for a sneak peek
at the next book in Elizabeth Boyle's
Rhymes With Love series,

IF WISHES WERE EARLS

Coming soon from Avon Books

Harriet Hathaway has only one wish when it comes to love: to marry the Earl of Roxley. But wishing for his heart and keeping it, Harriet will soon learn, takes more than casting up a whispered desire to come a part... to a happily ever after.

Continue reading for a sneak peek
at the next book in Elizabeth Boyle's
Rhymes With Love series

If Wishes Were Earls

Coming soon from Avon Books

PROLOGUE

It is but one night, my truest, my dearest,
Miss Darby, but it is all I need to carry you into
the starry heavens of pleasure. I promise you this,
come with me and from this evening forth you
shall reign forever as the Queen of my Heart.

PRINCE SANJIT TO MISS DARBY
FROM *MISS DARBY'S RECKLESS BARGAIN*

The Masquerade Ball, Owle Park
August 1810

"Oh, there you are, Harry. I'm almost afraid to ask what the devil you are doing—"

Miss Harriet Hathaway looked up from her quiet spot on the patio to find the Earl of Roxley standing in the open doorway.

Some hero! Oh, he might look like Lancelot, what with his elbow-length chain mail glittering in the light, his dark blue surcote and the leather breastplate trimmed with gold that seemed to accent both his height and breadth, but he'd taken his bloody time showing up to rescue her. It had been hard enough slipping out so that only he noticed.

And even then it had taken him a good half hour to come find her.

"Oh, Roxley is that you?" she feigned. "I hardly recognized you."

"Wish I could say the same about you," he said, his brow furrowed as he examined her from head to toe. "I've been sent by my aunt, oh, Queen of the Nile, to determine if you are awaiting Caesar or Marc Antony."

She'd spent most of the night dancing with rogues and unsuitable *partis*, waiting for him to intervene, and now he had, only he hadn't really . . . it had been by his aunt's bidding that he'd come to claim her.

Yet Harriet wasn't one to wallow in the details. For here he was, and this was her chance.

"Caesar or Marc Antony, you ask? Neither," she told him. "I find both quite boring."

"They wouldn't find you so," he said, stepping down onto the patio and looking over her shoulder at the gardens beyond. "You've caused quite a stir in that rag, minx."

Harriet turned around, and grinned. "Have I?" Of course, she'd known that the moment she donned the costume. And had very nearly taken it right off and sought refuge in some milkmaid's garb. But once Pansy, her dear friend Daphne's maid, had done Harriet's dark tresses up into an elaborate maze of braids, crowned them with a golden coronet of entwined asps and painted her eyes with dark lines of kohl, Harriet had known there was no turning back.

Roxley had come to stand beside her at the edge of the

patio. Here, away from the stifling air of the ballroom, the soft summer breezes, tinged as they were with the hint of roses, invited one to inhale deeply.

It was magical. Well, nearly so, she discovered.

The earl glanced over at her again and frowned. "You shouldn't be out here alone."

"I'm not," she pointed out. "You're here. But I had thought to take a turn in the gardens." Then she looked over at him again, standing there with a moody glower worthy of Lancelot. "Whatever is the matter?" she asked, hands fisting to her hips.

"It's that . . . that . . . costume you've got on," he complained, his hands wavering in front of her.

"It was supposed to be Daphne's."

That did not seem to appease him. "I cannot believe my aunt allowed you out in that shameful rag."

So much for magic.

"There is nothing wrong with this gown," she told him. "It is as historical as yours."

Good heavens, I'm wearing more than I was when you kissed me in Sir Mauris's garden, she wanted to remind him.

Then again, perhaps the kiss hadn't been as memorable to Roxley as it had been to her . . . Her gaze flew up, only to find his face a glower.

"Historical, indeed! Mine covers me," he replied. "No wonder Marc Antony lost his honor."

Harriet brazened her way forward. Better that than consider that Roxley had no interest in kissing her again. "Perhaps I should go find him and see if he will walk with me in the gardens." Since the only Marc Anthony inside the ballroom was Lord Fieldgate, this managed to darken Roxley's scowl. For most of the evening, the resplendent and rakish viscount had done his utmost to commandeer Harriet's time, declaring her his "perfect Cleopatra."

Roxley, as it turned out, wasn't done complaining. "How convenient for Fieldgate that Miss Dale's untimely departure—"

"Elopement," Harriet corrected.

"That is still left to be seen," Roxley commented. "It is only an elopement *if* they marry."

"*When* they marry."

"So you insist," he demurred.

"I do," Harriet said firmly. Daphne would never have run off so if she hadn't been utterly positive that she was about to be wed. She just wouldn't. "Besides, Preston will see them married."

"The duke will do his level best. He just has to find Lord Henry and Miss Dale before her cousin interferes."

Viscount Dale. Harriet hoped his carriage tumbled off the road. He was a rather bothersome prig, and could very well put a wrench into Daphne's plans.

"True love can overcome all odds," she said most confidently. At least it always did in her Miss Darby novels. Besides, she had to look no further than Tabitha and Preston, or Lord Henry and Daphne, for her proof.

True love always won the day.

And now she and Roxley would have their chance . . . Harriet glanced over at him, searching for confirmation.

"True love?" he scoffed. "Harry, you astound me. Now,

here I've always thought you the most sensible, practical girl I've ever known, but—"

The earl continued on, though Harriet had stopped listening at that one wretched word.

Girl. Though *sensible* was nearly as bad.

Would he ever stop thinking of her as a child? He certainly hadn't thought her merely a girl when he'd kissed her back in London.

Had he changed his mind since then? He couldn't have. He'd kissed her, for heaven's sakes. He wouldn't have done that unless . . .

She shook her head at the doubts that assailed her.

The ones that had plagued her since their arrival here at the Duke of Preston's house party.

What if Roxley didn't think her worthy of being his countess. It was easy to think so when she compared herself to the rest of the company. Then it was all too easy to see she had faults aplenty.

A decided lack of a Bath education. Like a proper lady.

Not one provided by her brothers' tutor.

She laughed too loud.

Her embroidery was nonexistent. Much like her skills at the pianoforte and watercolors.

In short, she wasn't refined enough to be a countess.

Even Roxley's.

But perhaps those things didn't matter to him, she told herself for about the thousandth time.

And certainly there was one way to find out.

Harriet straightened slowly, and then tipped one shoulder

slightly, letting the clasp at her shoulder—the one which held up the sheer silken over-gown—slide dangerously close to coming off her. The entire gown was like that—illusion after illusion that it was barely on, wasn't truly concealing the lady beneath. For under the first layer of sheer silk was another one in a shimmering hue of gold and beneath that, another sheer layer. The wisps of fabric, one atop the other, kept the gown from being completely see-through, though when she'd first donned it, she had to admit, she'd felt utterly naked.

Now she wanted to see if Roxley thought the same.

She tilted her head just slightly and glanced up at him.

"Yes, well," he managed, his gaze fixed on her shoulder. He looked as if he couldn't quite make up his mind or not to intervene—because to save her modesty he would have to touch her.

So she nudged him along, dipping her shoulder just a bit more. Perhaps this was exactly how Cleopatra had gained her Antony—for even now, Roxley appeared transfixed, leaving Harriet with a dizzy, heady sort of feeling.

But just before her gown fell from her shoulder, the earl groaned, then reached out and caught hold of the brooch at her shoulder and pushed it back up where it belonged, his fingers sliding along her collarbone, her bare skin. His hand was warm, hard, steady atop her shoulder, and suddenly Harriet could imagine him just as easily plucking the brooch away . . .

And then he looked at her, and Harriet saw all too clearly the light of desire in his eyes. Could feel it as his hand continued to linger on her shoulder and knew it would be nothing for him to gather her in his arms and . . . and . . .

"Demmit, Harry—" he muttered, snatching back his hand and stepping off the patio.

More like bolting.

"Whatever is the matter?" She hoped she sounded slightly innocent, for she certainly didn't feel it. His touch had left her shivering, longing for something altogether different.

"I . . . that is . . . I need some air. Yes, that's it. I came out here to get some air."

"I thought you came out to find me." She let her statement drift over him like a subtle reminder. "Yes, well, if you just came out for air, that's most excellent. I was of the same mind." And with that, she followed him.

For she couldn't help herself.

He looked over his shoulder at her. "Harry—"

"Yes, Roxley?" she tried to appear as nonchalant as possible.

"You cannot come out here with me," he said, pointing the way back to the well-lit patio.

"Whyever not?" she asked, as if she hadn't the slightest notion what he was saying.

And he didn't look like he wanted to discuss the subject either. But he did anyway. "It wouldn't be proper."

"Proper?" She laughed as if he were making a joke. "Oh, bother propriety. How long have we known each other?"

"Forever," he grumbled.

"And have we ever indulged ourselves in anything scandalous?" She strolled toward him and then circled him like a cat.

Other than that kiss . . .

"Not entirely," he managed, sounding a bit strangled, as

he gaped at her, at her bare shoulder, and then just as quickly looked away.

Well, that was something of an admission. At least she hoped it was.

"So whatever is wrong with you escorting me into the garden for a bit of air, especially since you've promised my brothers to keep an eye on me—which you have, haven't you?"

"Well, yes—"

"Do you think they would prefer I go for a walk in the gardens with Lord Fieldgate?"

More to the point, Roxley, she wanted to say, *do you want me out there with that bounder?*

"Bother you to hell, Harry. No, they wouldn't like it."

Neither would she. "So?"

His jaw worked back and forth, so much so, he did look like Lancelot caught between his loyalty to his liege and something less honorable.

Harriet hoped the less honorable part would win.

And to her delight it did. For the most part.

Roxley muttered something under his breath, and then caught her by the elbow and tugged her down the path. "Come along. Just don't do that thing with your lashes again." He frowned at her. "If your mother could see you—"

"She's in Kempton."

"As should you be," Roxley said, more as a threat. "I blame my aunt. She should never have brought you to London." He glanced at her again. "It's changed you." Then he added, "And not for the better."

"I see nothing scandalous about taking a walk in the gardens. I did this earlier with Lord Kipps and there was nothing so very wrong there. Why, your aunt encouraged it."

"She did?" he said, sounding none too pleased.

They rounded the first corner and came to a complete stop, for there before them was a couple—a water nymph and her Neptune—entwined together beneath an arbor, kissing passionately, between murmured endearments and confessions.

My dearest, my darling—

Oh, however did you know it was me?

How could I not?

"You see," Roxley was saying once they were well past the scandalous pair. "You are far better off out here with me than with Fieldgate."

"Yes, I suppose." She let every word fall with abject disappointment.

This brought the earl to a halt. "You suppose? Do you know what the rogue would do out here? Alone with you?"

Harriet shrugged. Truly, he had to ask? She had five brothers. She knew exactly what Fieldgate would do given the opportunity.

Wasn't it much the same as what Roxley had done back in London? Granted he'd been a bit foxed that night.

Oh, good heavens. She'd nearly forgotten that. He had been foxed.

What if he didn't remember kissing her? Or worse, he didn't want to recall the evening. Harriet drew in a deep breath, knowing full well the only way to get Roxley to admit anything was to provoke him.

Just a bit . . .

"I suppose, being the horrible rake that he is, he would have tried to take advantage of me—" Harriet sighed as if it were the most delicious notion she'd ever considered.

"Most decidedly," Roxley said with a disapproving *tsk, tsk* and a shake of his head, as if that made him the hero.

"You truly think so?"

He huffed a sigh. "Of course he would. You wouldn't have made it past the patio before he'd have tried."

"Oh, that is excellent news," she said, catching up the hem of her gown, turning on one heel, and starting to march back toward the ballroom.

Roxley caught up with her about where the couple was still locked in each other's embrace. Discreetly—well, as much as one could—he tugged her back down the path. "Where were you going?" he whispered as he dragged her away.

"I would think my plan was obvious. At least to a rogue like you. I was going to find the viscount."

"Fieldgate?" Roxley couldn't have sound more shocked.

"Yes. Is there another lascivious viscount by the name of Fieldgate that I've missed?"

Roxley's jaw set as he marched her farther down the path, through the long column of plane trees that lined the way.

Harriet could only hope this was the path to ruin, much as the other young lady had found.

A very unladylike tremor of envy sprang up inside her.

"Why would you want that clod to take advantage of you?" Rowley was asking. No, demanding.

"Because I've merely been kissed—and that lady"—she said with nod over her shoulder—"who I believe is Miss Nashe—"

Now the earl's head swiveled. "I highly doubt that's—"

But then he must have realized that just as Harriet's costume was so very memorable, so was the one Miss Nashe was wearing—of course minus the feathered hem that had caused her so much trouble earlier in the week.

"Told you," Harriet said triumphantly once they were well out of earshot. "That is Miss Nashe and Lord Kipps."

She held back an indignant *harrumph*. Lord Kipps had walked her down this very path and hadn't tried to kiss her.

Then again, Harriet wasn't an infamous heiress like Miss Nashe. Just plain old Harriet Hathaway. A spinster from Kempton. With barely enough pin money for just that.

Pins.

Oh, why couldn't she have been born fair and petite like Daphne, or inherited a fortune like Tabitha?

Roxley was still glancing back at the entangled couple. "Then I suppose we can expect an announcement at midnight. Lucky Kipps. He's gone and borrowed my family motto."

"Ad usque fidelis?" Harriet said, thinking that "Unto fidelity" was hardly the translation for what was transpiring in the arbor.

"No, minx, our other motto. The one we Marshoms find more apropos."

"Which is?"

"Marry well and cheat often," he teased.

This took Harriet aback. "The Marshoms advocate cheating on their spouses?"

"No." He laughed. "Unfortunately, we tend to love thoroughly and for life. We're an overly romantic lot—we just make sure to fall in love with a bride with a fat purse. And when that runs out, then there is nothing left but living by one's wits. My parents were a perfect example."

"You mean your parents lived by cheating at cards?"

"Of course. If only to stay ahead of their debts."

"Then it's a terrible shame," Harriet said, looking back at Miss Nashe and realizing how convenient it was that she'd found her countess's coronet with that earl, and not Harriet's.

"What is?" her earl asked.

"Kipps catching Miss Nashe's eye before you could cast your spell on her . . . and her fat purse."

Roxley shrugged. They had come to a stop by one of the larger trees. "Actually, I'm quite distraught about her choice."

"You wanted to marry her?" Harriet reached out and steadied herself against the white trunk of the tree.

He laughed. "No, Kitten. I had no designs on the lady. But I wagered she'd corner Lord Henry."

Kitten. Harriet nearly sighed at the familiar endearment. It held so much promise. Like a daisy being plucked of its petals.

He loves me . . .

Harriet laughed, at him and her hopes. "You should stick to cheating at cards." She put her back to the trunk, leaning against it, and letting the solid strength of the tree support her.

"You still haven't answered my question." Roxley dug the toe of his boot into the sod.

Harriet glanced up. "Which was?"

He looked up at her. "Why the devil would you want to come out into the gardens with Fieldgate?"

"For the very simple reason that I want to be kissed. Properly, that is. By a man of some skill." Harriet let her gaze drift back once again toward the house, her insinuation landing precisely as she'd intended.

Spectacularly.

"Kissed properly? Of all the insulting . . ." he blustered.

Harriet laughed again, and realizing he'd been lured into a trap, Roxley laughed as well.

"Good God, Harry!" He pushed away from the tree. "You're going to be the death of me."

"Well, if you were to kiss me . . . *again* . . ."

"Which I won't," he shot back.

"If you insist." Harriet did her best to appear indifferent, as if his quick retort was the least of her concerns.

"I do."

Truly, did he have to sound so adamant? "But if you did—"

He paused. "Harry, you can stop right there. Kiss you? Once was enough."

Harriet whirled around on him. "Aha! So you do admit to kissing me."

His voice ran low, rumbled up from his chest, his words filled with longing. "How could I forget?"

She shivered, for it was longing she shared, one that resided in her heart, restless and tempting.

"But you are being ridiculous," he continued. "If I were to ruin you, your brothers would shoot me."

"If they were in a good humor," she conceded. Actually, all five of them would most likely insist on taking a shot.

Unfortunately, Roxley knew this as well, for he echoed her thoughts exactly. "And since I don't favor an untimely death by firing squad, I fear for tonight your desire to be kissed again is going to have to remain on the shelf."

Like her life. Like her chances of ever being loved.

Passionately. Her gaze slid back in the direction of the arbor.

Oh, it all seemed so patently unfair. And yet, a few months ago, she would never have considered such things possible. She had lived her entire life content in the knowledge that as a spinster of Kempton she would never marry, never be kissed, never . . .

And then, on that fateful day when Preston's carriage had broken down in Kempton and she'd seen Roxley after all that time apart, she hadn't been able to help herself, she'd begun to dream of the impossible.

So, after coming to London with Tabitha and Daphne, and seeing her two dearest friends find happiness in such unexpected ways—not just happiness, but *love*—she'd begun to hope.

And here she was, with the only man she'd ever desired, in this garden, under this moon, and why shouldn't she want to be kissed?

Again. And again . . .

"No one would have to know," she whispered. "No one would ever find out."

"Someone always does, Kitten," Roxley told her. He'd circled round the tree and now stood much as she did, leaning against the great trunk but on the opposite side, so the wide breadth separated them.

How she longed to cut it down, to make it so that nothing could keep them apart.

"There are no secrets in the *ton*," he added.

Well, she didn't care if the entire population of England, Ireland and Scotland knew. It wasn't like she was an heiress with prospects, or anyone else was going to come along and claim her.

But the real question was, would he?

"Roxley?"

"Yes, Harry?"

She pressed her lips together every time he called her that. Did he have to use that horrid name? But taking a deep breath, she dove in. "What do you see when you look at me?"

"Not much," he said. "If you haven't noticed it is rather dark out here."

She rolled around the tree, her fingers tracing over the rough bark as if seeking a clear path, until she was right beside him. "Oh, do stop being *him*. I deplore *him*."

"Him? Who?"

"You know very well who I mean." Harriet was losing patience with him. If he pushed her much further she would go find Fieldgate. "Stop being the fool all London takes you for."

"But he's quite a handy fellow, that fool."

"He's an annoying jinglebrains."

"That's the point, minx."

"I know *who* you are."

"Do you?" He'd turned a bit and whispered the question into her ear.

Her breath caught in her throat, so that she was only able to answer with one word. "*Yes.*"

Oh, yes, she knew who he was. The only man who had ever made her heart beat like this.

And then he moved closer, brushing against the hem of her gown, and Harriet clung to the tree to steady herself. "No one would believe you, Kitten."

Kitten. Not Harry, but Kitten. His Kitten.

Harriet looked up at the bit of the night sky peeking through the thick canopy of leaves overhead and spied a single star. A lone, twinkling light. And so she wished.

"You don't have to hide from me," she whispered.

It was an invitation, one she knew he desired. She'd seen his struggle for months now—this game he played, this role he lived. This capering fool. Society's ridiculous gadfly.

But that wasn't the man she knew. The man she'd kissed in Sir Mauris's garden in London. The earl she'd known since they were children.

No, the one she loved, adored, desired, was the one with his gaze fixed on hers, his jaw set as if he were determined to do the right thing.

Oh, he'd chosen the right costume for the night. Lancelot. A man conflicted by duty and passion.

And he told her as much, his words almost desperate. "Why did you have to grow up, Harry? Why couldn't you have stayed in Kempton—stayed my impossible imp?"

"I still am."

"Oh, you are, but in an entirely new and utterly impossible way."

"Why is it impossible, Roxley?" *It certainly wouldn't be if you would but kiss me.*

"I promised your brothers I'd keep an eye on you."

Harriet moved closer, caught hold of his lapels and did the impossible, even as she whispered, "Then close your eyes."

CHAPTER ONE

*I have seen one night be the ruin
of many a good man.*

LT. THROCKMORTEN TO MISS DARBY
FROM *MISS DARBY'S RECKLESS BARGAIN*

London, April 1811
Eight months later

Every gambler knows the moment when his luck changes.

And not for the good. Luck is too fickle of a lover to whisper in a gamester's ear to encourage him to double down.

No, when she turns her back on a fellow, he knows it. As sure as all the air in the room has rushed out.

Like a fish out of water, he suddenly finds himself grasping at anything that might return her bright favor to his dark and empty pockets.

So it was with Tiberius Maximus Marshom, the 7th Earl of Roxley.

Roxley, who took wagers that no one else would, and won . . . The earl who always had pockets of vowels that only needed collecting was now dodging friends and ducking out of White's to avoid the embarrassment of his current dire financial straits.

And his shocking turn of luck was what had brought him here. To the City. To the offices of one Aloysius Murray.

"So you see, my lord," the merchant was saying, his hands folded atop a pile of notes, "you have no choice but to make my daughter your wife."

The earl looked across the wide expanse of the man's desk at a fellow he hadn't even known existed until two days ago when he'd received Mr. Murray's summons. Still, despite the gravity before him, Roxley could not resist smiling.

It was all he could do. A Marshom through and through, he knew he was trapped, but he was certainly not going to let this mushroom, this Mr. Murray with his most likely equally uncouth daughter, know that he had Roxley in a corner.

Mr. Murray pushed the papers across the top of the desk. "I've managed to buy out all your vowels, all your debts. You're solvent, for the time being. I think a kindly given 'thank you' would be in order." He paused for a moment and then added belatedly, "My lord."

Roxley looked at the pile of notes and scribbled promises and realized that his hopes of reclaiming all that he'd managed to lose over the past eight months—his money, his position with the Home Office, his standing (what there had been of it)—was for naught.

His legendary luck was gone.

If he were inclined to be honest—which he rarely was—he could point to the exact moment when Fair Fortune had abandoned him.

Eight months ago. The third of August, 1810, to be exact. The night he'd kissed Miss Harriet Hathaway.

And since we've established that the Earl of Roxley possessed very little honesty, kissing had been the least of his sins that night with the aforementioned Miss Hathaway.

He'd demmed well ruined her.

But enough of contemplating an evening of madness—it wasn't his insatiable desire for Harriet that had gotten him into this mess.

Oh, Harry what have I done? he thought as he looked at his all his wrongdoings piled up atop this *cit's* desk and knowing that no matter how much he . . .

Well, admitting how he felt for Harriet Hathaway was just too much honesty for one day. Especially this one.

When he was having to face his ruin. A reckoning of sorts.

If it was only the money, only his own ill-choices, that would be one thing. But there was more to this than just a gambler's reversal. His every instinct clamored that this was all a greater trap, a snare, but why and how, he couldn't say.

More to the point, he couldn't let this calamity touch anyone else.

As it had Mr. Ludwick, his man of business. Roxley's gut clenched every time he thought of the fellow—disappearing in the middle of the night with a good portion of Roxley's money.

Yet Ludwick wasn't the sort. And that was the problem. There was no explanation for his abrupt departure. None.

Further, the man's vanishing act had been followed by the revelation of a string of soured investments. Wagers began going bad. Files for the Home Office stolen from his house.

None of it truly connected, yet he couldn't help feeling that there was a thread that tied it all together, winding its evil around his life.

But who was pulling it, and why, escaped Roxley entirely.

Sensing the earl's hesitancy, Mr. Murray pressed his case, pulling out a now familiar document.

The mortgage on Foxgrove.

The one property of his that wasn't entailed. The one with all the income that kept the Marshoms afloat. Without Foxgrove . . .

Mr. Murray ran a stubby, ink-stained finger over the deed. "I've always fancied a house in the country. How is this village? This Kempton?"

"Kempton, you ask?" Roxley replied, wrenching his gaze up from the man's covetous reach on his property. "Oh, you won't like it. Cursed, it is."

Mr. Murray stilled at this, then burst out in a loud, braying laugh. "I was told to expect you to be a bit of a cut-up, but that! Cursed, he says." He laughed again, more like brayed.

Good God, Roxley could only hope Murray's daughter didn't laugh like that. But to keep Foxgrove . . . to keep his family out of debtor's prison, Roxley knew he could bear almost anything.

And if he did his utmost to make this mushroom's daughter miserable for the next forty years, he'd never have to hear that sound again.

That was, if anything, a small condolence.

"I have a mind to drive down next week," Mr. Murray was saying. "Probably needs renovations like the rest of the piles of stones you gentry keep."

Roxley ruffled at this. For his residences were his pride and joy. As had been his infamous luck that had kept them in good order. "Yes, well, currently my Aunt Essex lives at Foxgrove and she would be most put out to have strangers arrive at her residence."

"Isn't really hers, now is it?" Mr. Murray pointed out, once again running his ugly fingers along the edge of the deed.

He didn't even want to think about it. Aunt Essex forcibly removed from the house she'd lived in most of her life. She'd have no choice but to move permanently to London.

Into the earl's house. And without the income from Foxgrove, Aunt Eleanor in Bath, and Aunts Ophelia and Oriel at the Cottage would soon be forced to follow. All of the Marshom spinsters together. In one house. His house.

Worse than that, he'd have failed them. When they had once rescued him in his darkest hours.

He must have twitched as Mr. Murray chuckled. "Got your attention now."

"Mr. Murray, you had my full attention when you sent me the list of my debts you were holding. But what I don't understand is, why have you chosen to invest in me?"

Now it was Mr. Murray's turn to still, as if he wasn't too sure which direction to turn. But he had an answer at the ready soon enough. "Always fancied my daughter a lady, and a countess seems the right place to start."

Roxley nearly asked if the merchant was planning on sending him to an early grave, if only to climb the noble ladder again and gain a duke for his daughter the next time around.

"And," Murray added, as if suddenly finding the rest of his answer, "your situation is not unknown."

Roxley sighed. That was the truest thing the man had said since the earl had entered his study.

His fall from grace and rapid descent into debt had every tongue in London wagging. Hadn't he once told Harry as much?

There are no secrets in the ton.

So the word had spread quickly that the Earl of Roxley was up the River Tick.

Worse, to those who'd lost to him over the years, it was a just reward to watch. And since that was most everyone, the entire *ton* seemed delighted by his plummet.

"It's my daughter or the poorhouse with your aunts, my lord." Murray smiled as he folded his hands atop what was the ruin of Roxley's fortunes. "The choice is yours."

After the earl departed Mr. Murray's study, a door concealed by a bookcase opened, and a tall, darkly clad figure stepped out.

"I did as you instructed," Mr. Murray hurried to say. "But he won't agree to the marriage, my lord, until he meets my daughter."

"He'll agree," the man said with his usual supreme confidence.

A confidence that made Murray anxious. He didn't like being part of all this. Blackmailing a member of the House of Lords. It was bad business all around.

But so was the man before him.

"I did as you said—" Mr. Murray repeated.

The man arched a dark brow and studied him. "Yes, you did. Perfectly."

"Now the matter of that other issue . . ." The one that had brought Murray to the attention of this very dangerous stranger.

The man shook his head with a negligent toss of dismissal. "No. Not yet."

"But I—" Then Murray stopped as the man's brow arched upward.

Roxley's last man of business, Ludwick, had gone missing. Never been found. Nor had Roxley's money. Murray had known the man personally. Ludwick had always seemed an honest sort and certainly not the kind willing to embezzle a fortune and leave his wife and three children behind.

Murray looked up and met the other man's gaze. A cold shiver ran down his spine, as if this fellow could read his thoughts, the questions behind his silence.

"Yes, you have done all I've asked," the man assured him ever so smoothly. Like a knife in the dark sliding between one's ribs. "You bought up all of Roxley's debts and you've cornered him into this marriage"—he paused for a second— "to your delightful daughter. But our agreement will be concluded when he, and those accursed relations of his, are driven to ground and give me what is *mine*."

The malice in that one single word left Murray with the uncomfortable feeling that he was about to soil his own drawers. He chose his next words carefully.

Very carefully.

"You must despise the earl quite a bit to go to all this trouble." He waved a hand at the pile of notes on his desk—debts and misfortunes, Murray had no doubt, orchestrated by this deadly foe. "You must truly hate him, my lord."

"Hate Roxley?" the man laughed. "How droll. In truth, I count him a friend."

Eight long months. Harriet tapped her slipper impatiently. Eight months since that unforgettable night at Owle Park and the even more memorable day which followed.

When she'd discovered Roxley had fled.

Deserted the house party.

Abandoned her.

She could continue to list his failings, but that, she'd discovered over the fall and winter that had followed with not a single word from him, hardly served.

It only reopened the wound that had torn her heart in half.

She did her best to hold the broken parts together, yet it was as if the wound was still fresh and new, filled with festering doubts.

Oh, why had she agreed to come to London?

As much as she wanted to know why Roxley had abandoned her—oh, bother, she *must* know—she wasn't too sure she wanted to hear the truth.

But there had been Lady Essex, arriving at the Pottage and insisting that Harriet travel with her to London and Harriet's mother happy to oblige.

The two of them had packed her traveling trunks and shoved her aboard the Marshom barouche before she'd had a chance to rally a decent objection.

Certainly the truth wasn't an option.

Maman, Lady Essex, I have no desire to go to London and face the man who ruined me. Oh, yes, that would have been well received.

So here she was, about to do just that—see Roxley—and whatever would she say to him?

Perhaps she could ask this Madame Sybille everyone was fawning over—a mentalist or some such nonsense. All Harriet knew was that the lady had all the matrons buzzing when she'd arrived tonight. Perhaps this mystic could read her future and reassure her that Roxley's desertion was naught but a misunderstanding.

Harriet made an inelegant snort that drew a few censoring looks. Well, honestly, she didn't need some charlatan's advice, she needed help.

Glancing around, she pursed her lips. Where the devil was Tabitha? Or even Daphne, for that matter. They would know what to do.

Of course, that would also mean telling them . . . Harriet didn't know if she could bear the shame of it.

And then, as if on cue, there was a ruffle of whispers through the crush of guests.

Harriet had to guess that not only was Tabitha here, but her infamous husband as well.

She glanced at the steps leading down into the ballroom to find the happily married Duchess of Preston standing with her arm linked in the crook of her husband's elbow. Tabitha had defied all conventions and won the heart of the most unlikely of rakes.

Speaking of rakes, the duke and duchess had not arrived

alone. Preston stepped aside and was joined at the entrance by his uncle, Lord Henry Seldon, who grinned at the matrons who regarded him and his bride with abject horror.

Daphne's happiness rather defied the oft-repeated admonitions to young ladies all over proper society that nothing good ever came of a runaway marriage.

The former Miss Daphne Dale, now Lady Henry, flaunted evidence quite to the contrary. For not only was she gowned in a most fetching silk, her slightly wicked smile said her runaway union was very satisfying . . .

Harriet sighed with relief, feeling as if part of her burden was lifted. She had missed her dear friends ever so much. With Tabitha and Daphne married and living in London and at their husbands' various estates, Harriet had found herself alone in Kempton, the distant village where the three of them had grown up.

Of course, not even Kempton was the same. It had been decades since a Kempton spinster had even dared to marry, let alone the centuries that had passed since one had made a marriage that hadn't ended with the bridegroom meeting a horrific and untimely ending.

Usually on his wedding night.

And for several months after Tabitha and Daphne had married, it seemed every miss in the village had held her breath waiting for some disaster to befall Lord Henry or the Duke of Preston, or, heaven forbid, their brides.

But when neither Tabitha nor Daphne had gone mad and dashed their husbands over the head with a fire poker, there had been an emergency meeting of the Society for the Temperance and Improvement of Kempton.

Rising to her feet, the most esteemed of all the spinsters, Lady Essex, declared the curse broken.

"However can that be?" Miss Theodosia Walding asked, pushing her spectacles back up onto her nose. A bluestocking through and through, Theodosia liked her facts.

"Love," Lady Essex announced.

"True love," Lavinia Tempest corrected, her twin sister, Louisa, nodding in agreement.

The rest of the spinsters, who of course had heard Lavinia—one always heard Lavinia before one saw her—sighed with delight, while Theodosia frowned. She found such a fickle emotion as love or as ethereal as "true love" rather impossible to believe.

Yet, wasn't the proof before them? Tabitha and Daphne happily married. The curse must be ended and now it was time for all the spinsters, daughters and misses of Kempton to do what had been unthinkable before: prepare a glory box and make a match.

The rush at Mrs. Welling's dress shop had been akin to a stampede.

Not that Harriet had gotten caught up in the furor.

No, Harriet Hathaway's heart had been lost months earlier and all the evidence suggested he'd forsaken her.

No, he couldn't have. Not Roxley, she told herself.

It was an endless refrain she couldn't get out of her head.

He loves me. He loves me not.

She rose up on her tiptoes to look over Preston's tall shoulders to see if his party included one more.

Roxley.

But to her chagrin, there was no sign of the earl. No hint

of his devil-may-care smile, his perfectly cut Weston jacket, or that sly look of his that said he was working on the perfect quip to leave her laughing.

Bother! Where the devil was he? Harriet's slipper tapped anew.

"Harriet!" Tabitha called out, rushing toward her and wrapping her into a big hug. They had been best friends since childhood, and had never been separated for so long. "How I have missed you."

"And I you," Harriet confessed. Unfolding herself from Tabitha's warm embrace, she smiled at Daphne. "And you as well."

"Truly, Harriet?" Daphne said, waving her off. "I doubt very much you've missed me chiding you about the mud on your hem."

Harriet pressed her lips together to keep from laughing. Truly, she hadn't missed Daphne's exacting fashion standards. Still, she hugged her anyway, and to her surprise, Daphne hugged her back.

"I've missed you," her friend confessed. "You and your horrible Miss Darby novels."

Harriet dashed at the hot sting of tears that seemed to come out of nowhere. It wasn't until this moment that she realized just how lonely Kempton had become without Tabitha at the vicarage and Daphne down the lane at Dale House.

How much she wanted to tell them . . . and yet couldn't.

"The Miss Darby novels are not horrible," she shot back, more out of habit than not. "I just got the latest one. *Miss Darby's Reckless Bargain.* You *must* read it. Both of you. She's been captured by a Barbary sultan, a prince actually, and he's about to—" Harriet came to a stop as she found her friends pressing their lips together to keep from laughing over her earnest enthusiasm for her beloved Miss Darby.

Preston and Lord Henry, after exchanging a pair of befuddled glances, begged off and went to find where Lord Knolles kept something stronger than lemonade.

"Oh, don't look now, Tabitha, but Lady Timmons is here," Daphne said, nudging the duchess in the ribs.

"My aunt won't come over here as long as you are beside me, Daphne," Tabitha replied, and rather gleefully so.

"Whyever not?" Harriet asked, glancing over at Lady Timmons, who stood across the ballroom encircled by her three unmarried daughters. With a duchess for a niece, it made no sense that the lady wouldn't be cultivating Tabitha for introductions.

"She considers Daphne a bad example," the duchess confided. "She wrote me that it was imperative I sever my friendship with Lady Henry or else she couldn't, in good conscience, acknowledge me."

"Then I suggest you stay close at hand for Tabitha's sake," Harriet told Lady Henry. They all laughed again, for Lady Timmons had done her best to prevent Tabitha from marrying Preston, then had conveniently forgotten her objections to the match once she could claim a connection to a duchess.

As Tabitha and Daphne begged Harriet for news of Kempton—the most recent antics of the Tempest twins, Theodosia's newest scholarly pursuits, Lady Essex's latest complaints—Harriet noticed something else.

She looked from Tabitha to Daphne. "Why didn't you tell me?" she nearly burst out, looking at the swell of their stomachs, Tabitha's far more advanced than Daphne's.

"You know these things are not spoken of," Tabitha whispered, once again the vicar's daughter.

"Pish," Daphne said. "Men talk of breeding dogs and horses all the time! We mention a single thing about being in the family way and you would think we were asking them to walk down Bond Street without their breeches on!" She huffed a grand sigh. "Henry has gone so far as to forbid me from dancing—he won't have me exerting myself in any way." Her hands folded over the bulge. "He's become as fussy as Aunt Damaris, but I don't dare tell him that."

"Speaking of your Dale relations," Harriet said, "your mother actually mentioned your name the other day."

Daphne's parents had refused to acknowledge their daughter after she'd gone and eloped with a Seldon. Harriet never understood the point of it all, but to the Dales, the Seldon clan was akin to the devil. And vice versa. That their daughter had married one . . . well . . .

"Our happy news has helped, but I believe I have Cousin Crispin's recent match to thank for their changing opinion about my husband and his family."

"Then it's true," Harriet said. "Lord Dale has married her?"

Daphne covered her mouth to keep from bursting out with laughter. "Oh, he did. Mr. Muggins saw to that."

Tabitha, mortified over the part her dog had played in making Lord Dale's proposal of marriage—having locked the viscount and his unlikely choice in a wine cellar—changed the subject. "Is it true the Tempest twins are coming to London for the rest of the Season?"

Harriet nodded. "Yes. They'll be here in a fortnight. Their godmother, Lady Charleton, is sponsoring them."

"Lady Charleton?" an old matron who was standing nearby blurted out. "Did you say Lady Charleton?"

"Aye, ma'am," Harriet replied.

"Can't be right. Lady Charleton died . . . What is it now?" She turned to the even more ancient crone beside her. "When was it that Lady Charleton died?"

"Two years now. So sudden it was," the other woman said, shaking her head, leaving the yellow plumes in her turban all atwitter. "Dreadful situation still."

"Lady Charleton is dead?" Harriet shook her head. "I must have the name wrong."

"You must." The old lady turned back to her cronies and began clucking about yet another misfortune.

"Speaking of sponsors, where is Lady Essex?" Tabitha asked, glancing around them as if to gauge who else was eavesdropping on their conversation.

"Have you missed her as well?" Harriet teased.

Daphne and Tabitha both laughed. The spinster was a bit of a holy terror, not that Harriet minded.

"Some old roué swept her off her feet the moment we arrived," Harriet said. "Called her 'Essie.'"

"No!" Tabitha gasped.

"Yes!" Harriet nodded. "A Lord Whenby, I think his name is."

The three of them looked over at the eavesdropping old lady, but the name didn't elicit a response.

Daphne leaned closer. "Who is he?"

Harriet shrugged. She'd never heard Lady Essex mention the man. "I don't know. Perhaps that's why she's been at sixes and sevens for weeks now."

At this, Tabitha and Daphne exchanged a wary glance, one that suggested they might have quite a different explanation.

Harriet kept going, for now her interest was piqued. "I didn't think she was even going to come up to London this Season, but she arrived a few days ago at the Pottage and insisted my mother pack my bags."

There was yet another silent exchange between Daphne and Tabitha, but before Harriet could dig deeper into whatever *on dit* they were hiding, they were joined by a less than welcome guest.

"Miss Hathaway? Is that you?"

Harriet cringed at the familiar masculine voice.

"Do my eyes, nay, my heart, deceive me?" An elegantly dressed man in a dashing coat and well-glossed boots stopped before them.

She pasted a quick smile on her lips. "Lord Fieldgate," she acknowledged before dipping into a curtsy.

When she rose, he immediately caught hold of her hand and brought it to his lips. "My long-lost Hippolyta."

Daphne leaned over to Tabitha. "Hippolyta?"

"Queen of the Amazons," the duchess whispered back.

Daphne snorted.

"Roughly translated it means 'an unbridled mare.'" Tabitha's education by her vicar father always came in handy in situations like this.

Daphne pressed her lips together to keep from laughing.

"Yes, exactly," Tabitha remarked. "If only the viscount knew how close to the mark his title for Harriet is."

Harriet shot them both a sharp glance. *It isn't as if I can't hear you.*

"I must beg a dance of you," Fieldgate continued. Nor had he let go of Harriet's hand. "No, make that two." Oh, no one could say the viscount lacked charm, for his smile smoldered with promise, a sort of smoky glance that could make a lady go weak in the knees.

"Two?" Harriet shook her head at her ardent suitor who had pursued her so steadily the previous Season. Apparently absence had not dimmed Fieldgate's ardor.

"The supper dance, at the very least," he pleaded.

The supper dance? Harriet's pique returned. Roxley would deplore that. He had hated it every time she'd danced with the viscount last Season.

Then again, it would serve the earl right to have to partner some leftover debutante to supper, especially after all these months of silence on his part.

Her heart gave a familiar leap into that horrible abyss over which she'd been teetering for months.

He loves me, he loves me not.

Well, tonight, she'd discover the truth. If she had to carve it out of the cursed man with one of the ancient broadswords mounted on the wall. Manacle him to a sideboard and . . . why, she'd . . .

And then Harriet stopped. For indeed the entire world seemed to stop all around her. For across the room, off to one side, she saw him.

Roxley.

He *was* here. Had been here for some time, for there he was holding court in the far corner.

He loves you, he loves you not, her heart prodded.

"Can I take your silence to mean you're granting me the supper dance . . ." Fieldgate's words were both encouraging and full of confidence.

Harriet barely heard him, her heart hammering wildly. Roxley. With the crush of guests, she'd nearly missed him, but the crowd had parted for a moment and in that magical instant she'd spotted him. The cut of his jaw, the wry smile she loved.

Her breath stopped, as it had when his lips had teased across the nape of her neck. His hands had caressed her, *all of her,* and she'd trembled then as she was trembling now.

"A mistake, Kitten. This is ever so wrong," he'd whispered *that night at Owle Park even as his head had dipped lower, his lips leaving a trail of desire down her limbs.*

Oh, please don't let it all have been a mistake, she told herself yet again. Harriet took a step toward the earl without even thinking, pulled by the very desire he'd ignited that night, forgetting even that the viscount still held her hand.

Roxley loves me.

Or loves you not, that dangerous voice of doubt whispered back.

"You cannot refuse me, my queen, my Hippolyta," Fieldgate continued, all gallant manners, though he might as well have been grasping at straws.

"Yes, yes," she said absently, glancing quickly back at him before plucking her hand free. Meaning, *Yes, I can refuse you.*

But the viscount took her words for assent and grinned in triumph.

"Harriet, there is something we need to tell you—" Tabitha began, reaching out to stop her, but Harriet sidestepped her grasp.

"Yes, dear, you must listen," Daphne continued like a chorus.

If they were going to warn her off from spending too much time in the roguish viscount's company, they needn't bother. She had no intention of spending another second with Fieldgate.

Not with Roxley so close at hand. She'd have her answers, he'd apologize profusely, sweep her off her feet and marry her as soon as a Special License could be procured.

That was how it always happened.

In fiction, her sensibilities reminded her.

"Harriet, please," Daphne called after her.

She ignored her. Truly, whatever they had to say could hardly matter, but just in case, Harriet hurried a bit, only to find her path blocked by her brother Chaunce.

Oh, pish! Was there ever a girl more overly blessed with bothersome and meddlesome brothers than she?

And Chaunce, her second oldest sibling, had that look of unrelenting determination about him.

All the Hathaways were determined, but Chaunce's tenacity came with all the solid warmth of a brick wall.

In December.

"Harry," he said, bussing her warmly on the cheek. "There you are. Mother wrote that she thought you would arrive in time to attend tonight."

Harriet was not deceived. He hardly looked thrilled to be attending Lady Knolles's soirée, rather more like the bearer of bad tidings.

Couldn't Chaunce, just once, leave well enough alone and just enjoy the world?

Just as Harriet meant to once she was reunited with her beloved Roxley.

"And so I have," she told her brother. "But I must—"

Chaunce glanced over his shoulder and spied the direction of her determination. If anything, his grim smile now turned into a hard line. "That won't do, Harry. You can't just run after him. Not now—"

Freeing herself from him, she patted her brother on the arm and circled around him, dodging his grasp. "You've become as stodgy as George," she chided. "Roxley is our dear friend. I am merely greeting him. He'll be delighted to see me."

He'd better be . . .

"Harry—" Chaunce continued as she slipped again into the crowd before he could stop her.

"No, Harriet! Don't. Not just yet," Tabitha called after her, having finally caught up.

But there was no stopping Harriet now.

Mr. Chauncy Hathaway turned around and frowned at his sister's friends. "You didn't tell her?"

"We hadn't the time," Daphne replied.

Chaunce groaned, raking a hand through his dark, tousled hair. "How long does it take to tell someone that the man she loves is marrying another?"

About the Author

ELIZABETH BOYLE has always loved romance, and now she lives it each and every day by writing adventurous and passionate stories that readers from all around the world have described as "vastly entertaining" and has been publishd in 1996, she won the book become *New York Times* and *USA Today* bestsellers and won the RWA RITA® Award and *Romantic Times* Reviewers Choice Awards. She reads just as a great-uncle husband and two sons for hours in reading in the time to call them. Readers can visit her on the Web at www.elizabethboyle.com.

Visit www.AuthorTracker.com for exclusive information on your favorite HarperCollins authors.